My Imperfect Love

Niharika Jindal is a 30-year-old writer from Ahmedabad. After spending four years studying Psychology in Claremont McKenna College, California, she returned to India clueless about her next step. She started with a few stints in human resources, during which she met her husband on an arranged coffee date, and it was love at first sight.

After many drives and dinner dates, Niharika is now happily married. However, her fairy tale was cut short when she developed a chronic back condition—which she has been battling ever since. Constantly trying to figure out a way to take her mind off the pain, her saving grace came in the form of reading, her favourite childhood pastime. She decided to give writing a shot.

Niharika's debut novel, *Wake Up, Girl!* was published in November 2018. The book was an instant success, and was in the Amazon bestseller list within two weeks of its release. Various influencers and Bollywood personalities have featured it on social media platforms across the country since then.

In her free time, Niharika can be found reading, listening to romantic songs, having cold coffee, shopping online, catching up with old friends, doing physiotherapy and binge watching television shows with her husband.

My Imperfect Love

Niharika Jindal

Published by
Rupa Publications India Pvt. Ltd 2023
7/16, Ansari Road, Daryaganj
New Delhi 110002

Sales centres:
Allahabad Bengaluru Chennai
Hyderabad Jaipur Kathmandu
Kolkata Mumbai

Copyright © Niharika Jindal 2023

This is a work of fiction. Names, characters, places and incidents are either the product of the authors' imagination or are used fictitiously and any resemblance to any actual person, living or dead, events or locales is entirely coincidental.

All rights reserved.
No part of this publication may be reproduced, transmitted, or stored in a retrieval system, in any form or by any means, electronic, mechanical, photocopying, recording or otherwise, without the prior permission of the publisher.

P-ISBN: 978-93-5702-077-0
E-ISBN: 978-93-5702-043-5

First impression 2023

10 9 8 7 6 5 4 3 2 1

The moral right of the author has been asserted.

Printed in India

This book is sold subject to the condition that it shall not, by way of trade or otherwise, be lent, resold, hired out, or otherwise circulated, without the publisher's prior consent, in any form of binding or cover other than that in which it is published.

*To all the authors who made me fall in love
with the hero in every book I read...
I hope I manage to do the same for
all the girls who read this book!*

Prologue

2000

Boom! Boom! Target annihilated.

The computerized voice was making Saahil's head hurt, but he couldn't stop, now that he was finally so ahead in the video game. Quite aptly named *House of the Dead*, the zombie-killing game was all the rage.

Saahil checked the time on his computer screen and sighed. It was past 10.00 p.m. again, which his parents had decided was the correct bedtime for an eight-year-old.

What was the harm in a couple of minutes? No one had come to check on him, anyway.

Saahil trained his eyes to the game again and proceeded to defeat the next monster. He could hear voices coming from the nearby room. The noise level was particularly less tonight in comparison—there were times when even a pillow over the head couldn't do the job.

Okay, hold on. He'd spoken too soon.

'Goddamn it, Payal! I can't have this argument over and over!' Saahil's father shouted. 'I really don't understand the reason for your complaints! What don't you have? I've provided you with every single thing possible and you still manage to think of some godforsaken issue!'

'Well, I wouldn't have so many issues if you chose to come home sober once in a while, Manan! It's not even 10.00 p.m.

yet and I can smell the alcohol on you from a mile away! What sort of example are you setting for Saahil?' His mother countered.

Saahil cocked his head to the side. *Interesting.*

His name usually didn't come up during his parents' fights.

Saahil wondered if his parents knew that he could hear every single one of their arguments. Initially it had scared him slightly, but over the past year, the fights had been happening so frequently that he didn't even notice anymore.

You have successfully completed level 2.

Yes! He pumped his fist in the air.

'Can't you think of something new to say? I'm so sick and tired of your constant nagging, woman!' Manan's voice rose a bit further.

'You are such a child! I can't believe I married such an irresponsible man! You're good for nothing!' Payal shouted back.

Suddenly, there was a loud thud from his parents' room.

Saahil craned his neck to hear further but everything had gone quiet. He wondered what the thud had been. Maybe someone had tripped and fallen.

Oh, wait. He could now hear his mother's wails.

A couple minutes passed but Saahil couldn't hear anything more. No more conversations. He decided to go to bed just in case someone decided to come check on him.

As he lay in the darkness, Saahil tried to fall asleep.

Several minutes passed by.

A single tear rolled down his cheek, bringing all the demons of the night closer.

2004

'Payal, beta, calm down! Both of you need to sort this out.'

Saahil woke up to loud noises outside his bedroom door.

What the hell is happening?

Now that he was twelve and of a slightly cooler age, saying or thinking 'hell' was most definitely allowed.

He opened his door slightly and saw his parents staring daggers at each other across the living room. His grandparents were the referees for this particular shouting match.

Great. People have to turn on the television to watch *Mahabharata*, but it's something else to witness it right here every day in the living room.

'I can't stand the sight of him, Maa! Ask him what he was doing last night!' Payal shouted with tears rolling down her face.

This was definitely the wrong thing to say, because Manan took a step toward Payal with a murderous look on his face, 'Your fight is with me, Payal! Don't you dare drag my parents into this!'

Saahil's dada held up a hand and tried to stop Manan from saying anything more. For the very first time, Saahil observed that his grandfather was looking extremely old and haggard. Normally, the patriarch of the Kapoor household was a force to reckon with.

'Both of you, keep your voices down,' he said quietly. 'There's a way to handle things, haven't I taught you that, Manan?'

Hearing his words, Manan took a step back.

Way to go, Dada! You still got it.

Payal, however, was not one to remain quiet.

'You have no idea what has been going on right under

your noses all this time, Papa! This man—this filthy man—oh God, I need to sit down.'

Payal sank down on a nearby couch and put her head between her hands.

Saahil looked down at himself and realized that he was in his boxers. Recently, he had started sprouting hair all over his body and now keenly observed the smattering of light on his stomach hair.

No time other than now to notice body hair.

He wondered if anyone would even notice if he ran to the middle of the room and broke out in a bhangra routine.

Probably not.

There was a sudden scuffling from downstairs and then, a rapid succession of footsteps on the stairs. What happened next would always be a blur in Saahil's mind.

'Payal! Get up and pack your things! We are leaving!'

Saahil's maternal grandparents had now arrived on the battlefield.

This statement by Nana caused Manan to fly off his handle once again and start shouting, 'What do you mean, pack your things? She isn't leaving till I say she's leaving! Stop right there, Payal!'

Manan had blocked Payal from moving by now. 'She isn't leaving! Just try and make her leave!'

Payal was howling on top of her lungs, 'Let me go, Manan! I want to leave!'

A sudden noise that sounded eerily similar to a crack of a whip wafted through the room.

Nana had slapped Dad. Hard!

Saahil quietly shut the door behind him.

And all hell broke loose.

one

2015

Rhea Singh adjusted the lehenga on the model in front of her and let out a huge sigh. This model was being especially difficult. She was busy Snapchatting, trying on all the various filters that would make her look slightly prettier or sillier.

'Lights guy? Where's the lights guy?' Rhea shouted.

No one replied.

'Hey. You. Come here,' Rhea beckoned to an intern who was passing by. 'Hold this fabric right here. Oh, God, not like that. We've all been here for the past ten hours shooting for the brand catalogue, so it would help if you understood what I'm trying to say!'

The intern's face fell and Rhea immediately felt guilty. She was being a complete and total bitch.

She sighed again. It had been a long day.

'Excuse me, do you mind?' Rhea asked the model in exasperation.

'Huh? Oh, sorry, Rhea. What do I have to do?' The model replied innocently.

'Just…try not to move so much. I'll go find the lights guy and the photographer. Don't move,' Rhea emphasized again and dug the tiny safety pin that was holding the lehenga in position into the model's waist.

'Ouch! What the fuck was that!'

'I didn't do anything, I swear!' The intern replied, frightened.

Rhea stifled her giggle and went off to find the rest of the crew. This photo shoot had been going on long enough.

'Rhea? What do you think of these pictures? Mr Varma has asked us to finalize the best pictures by tonight,' a colleague ambushed her on the way.

'I can't see them right now. Have a slightly more troublesome situation to take care of,' Rhea replied as she hurried off to find her crew members.

Working under Kavita Mehta's banner had been more of a challenge than Rhea had anticipated. The designer's team was brilliant and Rhea had to bring her A game, every day, to be able to compete with the rest of her colleagues.

However, it was all going to be worth it. *One more week and you'll be on your way to London for graduate school*, Rhea told herself.

London College of Fashion had loved the designs that Rhea had submitted for their fashion design graduate programme. In fact, they had offered her a scholarship for the entire year along with accommodation.

No more poring over countless potential designs, no more long nights filled with model fittings, and definitely no more hemming waistlines. A break was imminent.

'Bharat? I've been waiting for you guys for the past fifteen minutes!' Rhea barked at the lights guy when she saw him in the back room.

He was obviously wasting time because he quickly hid his phone in his back pocket before answering, 'Sorry, Rhea, I was just heading to you.'

'And where the hell is the photographer?' Rhea asked in a frustrated tone.

'I'll find him as well,' Bharat replied and hurried off.

Just at that moment, one of the supervisors on duty came into the back room and smiled when she saw Rhea, 'Hey. Mr Varma wants to see you.'

Rhea groaned. *Really? Why right now?*

Muttering under her breath, Rhea knocked on the department head's office door, 'May I come in, Mr Varma?'

'Yes, Rhea, come on in,' came the reply.

The AC in the cabin provided a sudden jolt of relief to Rhea's senses. She suddenly felt refreshed.

'The AC feels good, huh?' Mr. Varma asked smilingly, noticing her expression relax.

'Sure does. Working late tonight?'

'Well, you know this time of the season is always busy. Sorry that I've been keeping you so late, Rhea. You're one of our most competent employees and I hate that you're leaving in a week,' Mr Varma stated.

Rhea chuckled nervously. This was a sticky situation. Management had been trying to lure her into staying with Kavita Mehta, but they weren't offering her a lucrative salary. Since she and her mother were in a bit of a sticky situation, financially, there was no reason for her to stick around in a low-paying job.

'I'm sorry, Mr Varma, but I believe a year-long course at London College of Fashion is the best move for me. I wouldn't turn down this offer otherwise. You know I've loved working here over the past year,' Rhea replied.

'Oh, well, I had to try. I wish you all the best, Rhea. Knock 'em dead. Now, go home. We've kept you here long enough.'

Rhea felt relief coursing through her while she walked over to her cubicle.

Finally, she was going home.

A scream brought Rhea out of her reverie. The model had tripped and fallen face-down on the carpeted floor.

Rhea turned her face away and let out a laugh. That fall would look swell on social media.

Elvis Presley's 'Jailhouse Rock' burst out from inside her bag and Rhea saw her mother's name flash on her phone.

'Hi, beta. What are we having for dinner tonight?' Simran Singh asked in a breezy tone.

'Mom. You know I hate that question.'

Rhea knew that her mother specifically asked her this question every single evening just to annoy her. It was part of their daily repartee. As much as it annoyed her, Rhea knew Simran couldn't help it. Ever since Rhea's father had passed away after a long illness five years ago, it had just been the two of them.

She tried to shake away the guilt taking over her body—her mother was going to be all alone once Rhea left for London.

'Doesn't mean you don't have to eat. Chinese take-out?' Simran prompted.

'Mom, one thing that Mumbai doesn't have is good Chinese take-out. Let's order Thai instead.'

'Okay. See you at home. Love you,' Simran said before hanging up.

Rhea had always been extremely close to her mother, but they had become inseparable ever since her father had passed away. His passing had taken its toll on Simran, but she tried to hide it as best as possible, for Rhea's sake.

Simran Singh was the strongest person that Rhea knew.

Changing cities had been good, though.

Delhi would always have too many memories

associated with her father. From the local eateries to all the neighborhoods—everything had a special significance. Rhea and her mother had welcomed the pleasant change that Mumbai had provided.

She took the elevator to the ground floor, and walked out to the busy street. Rhea finally managed to flag a taxi down and was soon on her way to their apartment in Andheri West.

The only difference between living in Delhi and Mumbai was the cramped living arrangement. It had been a year since they had moved to Mumbai, but they still weren't quite used to the apartment life. But neither of them spent much time there, in retrospect. Simran left for her job at an insurance company right about the same time Rhea left the apartment and they both returned late evening.

When she was about halfway home, there was a ping on her cell phone. A WhatsApp message from Simran:

```
Come soon. Just placed the order!
```

Rhea replied:

```
Almost there.
```

About twenty minutes later, the taxi stopped in front of the apartment building and Rhea quickly paid him. On the way to the elevator, she caught a sight of herself in the mirror and sighed.

I really need to go to one of those exorbitantly priced salons. 'Another week and you'll be the proud owner of one of those coveted unibrows, missy,' Rhea muttered to herself.

While her slim body seemed fine, her face looked pale and tired. Her eyes didn't need any kajal—the dark circles were doing all the work.

Simran opened the door on the first doorbell ring.

'There's the sunshine of my life, the apple of my eye, and the stars in my sky!' Simran enveloped Rhea in a big hug.

'Stop it, Mom,' Rhea laughed.

Seeing her mother was the perfect antidote for a long day. She and her mother could talk endlessly without making any sense at all and change gears in a heartbeat.

'Okay. How was work, baby? You look really tired,' Simran said in a concerned voice.

'Oh, it was long. That's the only word I would use to describe today, Mom,' Rhea replied.

'Only a week more and then you'll be off! Excited for the change you so deserve?' Simran asked with a smile.

'Yes. Can't wait. Though I'm really not excited to do everything by myself. You know I'm not the best caretaker when it comes to myself,' Rhea stated frowningly.

'Oh, you'll be fine, beta. You'll get the hang of it. Now, tell me what movie are we watching with our food? There's some new Akshay Kumar movie that's out,' Simran informed.

'Definitely not that. How about some old Hollywood movie? I feel like watching *Titanic*,' Rhea replied excitedly.

'You got it. You sort out the movie while I get all the plates out. The delivery guy should be here any second,' Simran hurried off.

Rhea started sorting through their DVD collection. They were both huge movie freaks. As the movie started to play on the screen, tears sprung to her eyes and she went to the kitchen where Simran was humming to herself.

'I'll really miss you, Mom,' Rhea said as she hugged her mother from behind. 'I'm sorry I'm leaving you and going.'

'Rhea! Stop this nonsense! You have to go and learn as

much as you can. I'll be fine, baby. Besides, when you're gone, I can finally lose all the weight that I've put on. While you may not gain a single kilogram, the rest of us actually need to exercise!' Simran exclaimed.

Rhea laughed, 'I love you.'

'I love you too. Now, go back to the living room. I think Leo's about to make his entry.'

two

'Rhea, you really need to chill out!' Neha shouted.

Rhea had finally reached London and was freaking out. This was the first time she'd ever been so far away from home and it was all getting to be a bit much to take in.

Her only saving grace had been Neha Agrawal, Rhea's school friend from Delhi and currently the only person that she knew in London.

'Oh, God, stop arranging all your books in alphabetical order!' Neha screamed.

'Oh. Sorry. Didn't realize I was doing that,' Rhea said sheepishly.

Arranging her books in alphabetical order had always been a stress buster for Rhea. Some people cleaned, some listened to music, she rearranged her books in alphabetical order.

They were in her dorm room, and to Rhea's horror, it was even smaller than her cramped room in Mumbai. It wasn't as if she was expecting something along the size of a grand ballroom, but *this* was beyond tiny. And dragging two big and heavy suitcases from the tube station to all the way up here had been a real task.

'Earth to Rhea. Where did you vanish?' Neha was waving her hands in front of Rhea's face.

'Stop doing that. You're making me dizzy,' Rhea groaned. 'Neha, what am I doing here? I don't belong here.'

'Rhea, you've been in London for a total of five minutes.

Stop complaining. Give it a couple of days and you'll see what an amazing place it is!' Neha declared.

London certainly agreed with Neha. Her awkward and lanky friend from school had transformed into an extremely beautiful and confident young lady.

Rhea took a deep breath, 'Yes, you're right. I'm just worried about Mom, I guess.'

She sat down on her new bed and started massaging her temples. It was the beginning of a headache.

Rhea couldn't help but fear that her mother would get incredibly lonely. Their last couple of days together had been bittersweet—neither had wanted to acknowledge the distance that was going to come between them soon.

'Dude, Simran aunty is an extremely strong and positive person. She'll be fine,' Neha stated reassuringly.

'Yeah, you're right. I'm just overthinking things,' Rhea sighed.

She wished she could just shut her brain and revel in the fact that she'd made it to London! If this wasn't a reason to celebrate, she didn't know what was.

'Okay, that's it. I can't see you moping around anymore. God knows what you're moping about in the first place. We're in London, baby! Grab your coat. We're going out,' Neha said firmly.

Rhea let out a short laugh, 'I'm not going anywhere. Look at the state of this room. I have a million things to do! Who the hell is going to unpack all this stuff?'

∞

London was spectacular. That was the only thought in Rhea's mind as she and Neha roamed around Covent Garden.

The energy of the place was fantastic—the bustling streets, the incredible weather, and not to mention, the sight of scrumptious food everywhere.

'Rhea, you've got to try these macarons,' Neha said suddenly.

She dragged Rhea off to a store called Ladurèe and the sight stunned her when they got there—mountains and mountains of macarons just stacked together for the world to see and enjoy.

So, this is what a mountain made out of sugar looked like. It looked better in reality than what Rhea had ever imagined.

'There's nothing better than this,' Neha said dreamily.

While Rhea was trying to get over the fortress of macarons in front of her, Neha quickly ordered a box of six.

'That'll be eighteen pounds, miss,' the sales guy stated.

Eighteen pounds! That was beyond expensive. Rhea's heart skipped a beat.

This was another thing that was stressing Rhea out.

How was she going to survive living in London on her budget?

She quickly handed Neha her share of nine pounds. These macarons had better be worth it.

'Here, try this one,' Neha handed Rhea a green-coloured pistachio macaron.

The bite melted into her mouth before she had even started chewing. It was that good.

'Told you London's worth it,' Neha smirked.

Neha's phone suddenly started to ring and she picked up, 'Hello? Hi. No, I'm at Covent Garden. Yes, I'm with my friend, Rhea.' She listened to whatever the person on the other end was saying and said before hanging up, 'Cool, see you soon.'

'Before you argue with me, let me just say that meeting a couple of people will be good for you. You'll feel slightly more at home,' Neha said with a hand held up in front of her like a traffic police officer.

Rhea knew there was no point in arguing with Neha. She decided to just go with the flow.

She said laughingly, 'Okay. Whatever you say, Sergeant, I'm here to obey. But, am I dressed okay?'

Rhea turned around in a circle for Neha to assess her simple top and jeans.

Neha snorted, 'Rhea, you could have just woken up, and still managed to look amazing. That face and body are to die for. Let's go.'

As they walked toward Baker Street, Rhea felt infinitely lighter. The crisp air of London was doing its job. She turned her face toward the setting sun and felt relaxed. She just hoped her first day at college goes well.

It was the beginning of a new life.

∞

The apartment on Baker Street was immensely loud.

There were at least thirty people jammed together in the tiny space. However, no one seemed to mind the close proximity and Rhea understood the reason soon enough. Several alcohol bottles stood on the table, most of them empty.

'Neha! You came!' A stylishly dressed girl in a short dress appeared out of nowhere and hugged Neha.

'Hi, Pooja! This is my friend, Rhea. The one I told you about,' Neha smiled warmly.

'Hi, Rhea. So nice to meet you,' Pooja hugged Rhea.

Okay, this girl is definitely into long hugs. Rhea awkwardly waited for it to end.

'What are the two of you going to have? We have everything. Come on, let's do a tequila shot,' Pooja said excitedly.

She dragged Neha and Rhea to the crowded bar in the corner of the apartment, and poured three tequila shots into shot glasses. Tequila was Rhea's new favourite drink. It resulted in much more tolerable hangovers than vodka and whiskey.

'To Rhea being in London!' Neha said with a big smile.

'To Rhea!' Pooja shouted and gulped down her shot at a shockingly fast pace.

'Thanks, guys,' Rhea said as she drank her own shot.

It went down smoothly and Rhea felt a slight burning sensation in her stomach.

Now, this, felt similar.

'Come on, Rhea, I'll introduce you to everyone,' Pooja slurred.

'Whoa, Pooja, maybe you should sit down first,' Neha laughed. 'There's plenty of time for introductions.'

Yes, Pooja really needed to sit down. She looked like she was about to make an imprint of herself on the carpeted floor any second.

There was a loud noise from behind them and they all turned around to see what had caused the commotion.

'A dare is a dare, dude! Stop being such a pussy,' said an incredibly drunk guy to an extremely scared looking guy.

'But-but I can't...'

There was a chorus of boos from around the room.

'Well, you should have thought of that before you entered this game of Truth or Dare. Now, you better do what you're supposed to or it's goodbye for you, buddy,' said the drunk guy arrogantly.

'N-No, I really can't, I'm sorry,' said the scared-looking guy.

Poor guy. Why are they being so mean to him?

'I feel so bad for him,' Rhea muttered to Neha.

'Ssshhh!' Neha whispered back.

'Let it be, Zahan. He's starting to cry now,' said a voice from somewhere, but Rhea couldn't see the person who had said it.

Oh, wait. There he was.

For a second, Rhea was momentarily speechless. Whoever this guy was, he had something about him. Broad built, with a five o' clock shadow on his face, he was exceptionally good looking. But, no, it wasn't just that. He had this air of confidence that made him look far superior than everyone around him. Rhea had rarely seen anyone who looked so sure of himself.

'But, Saahil, it's a dare…' said Zahan to the hot guy.

'Let it go, Zahan. He's about to wet himself,' Saahil stated.

And that was that. The entertainment of the evening was over.

The scared-looking guy bolted from the room. Rhea let out a sigh of relief on his behalf.

'Whew. He looked like he was about to pass out,' Rhea commented to Neha.

Just at that moment, Pooja let out a loud burp and put her hand to her mouth, 'I think I'm about to throw up!'

'Pooja! Bathroom! Now!' Neha grabbed a hold of Pooja's arm and started leading her away.

'Rhea! Entertain yourself, please. I'll be back soon,' Neha called out as she walked off.

'Don't worry! I'll be…fine,' Rhea said to no one.

Neha and Pooja were nowhere to be seen.

Great. She was all alone in this crowded chaos.

Rhea turned toward the bar and poured herself another shot of tequila.

'Care to share?'

Rhea turned around in a hurry, almost dropping her drink. It was none other than Mr Hot Guy.

three

Saahil Kapoor had a bad headache.

He'd been at Pooja's apartment for over an hour and was already bored out of his mind. Something had better change soon or else he was splitting.

'Saahil, would you like to get another drink? I was thinking of heading to the bar,' the blonde sitting next to him asked animatedly.

'Here,' Saahil handed her his empty glass. 'Whiskey and water. Thanks.'

The blonde's mouth fell open.

Saahil kept a straight face and watched her walk away. He knew he was being a jerk but he wasn't in the mood for dealing with a drunk girl at the moment. And the blonde was plenty drunk already.

It was the same scene over and over for as far as Saahil could remember—alcohol flowing and the night dragging on endlessly.

Initially, he had always been the last one to leave at any party. But now, it seemed to have lost its appeal.

Something needed to change.

Saahil was looking around the room, bored, when his eyes landed on the new girl.

I haven't seen her before, Saahil thought to himself. Because if he had, there was no way he would have forgotten that face.

Not bad. Not bad at all. The new girl was tall and slender, with hair that shone as it fell down her back. Saahil wondered if it was as soft as it looked.

Maybe the night wouldn't be so bad, after all.

Luckily for him, she was standing all by herself, looking slightly lost in the drunken crowd.

Since she was facing the other way, she couldn't see Saahil approaching her. He whispered almost next to her ear, 'Care to share?'

She turned around in such a hurry that she almost dropped her drink.

Her face was so expressive. Saahil saw a range of expressions on it in less than a second. *Must be nice to show all your feelings on your face. Or incredibly dumb.*

Saahil could see that he'd managed to rattle her.

Hiding his grin, he continued, 'Oh, shit, I'm sorry I snuck up on you like that. Let me pour you a new shot.'

Without waiting for her answer, Saahil took the shot glass from her hand.

'There's...no need for that,' she said.

'Of course, there is. A lady should never be with a glass half empty,' Saahil winked at her.

He saw her face turn red. *She really is expressive.*

'I'm being rude again. I'm Saahil,' he said with a smile.

'Yeah, I got that. You know, from that game earlier. You tried stopping the mean guy from harassing the scared guy... oh sorry, he's probably your friend,' she apologized, her face red again.

Saahil laughed. It was the first genuine laugh he'd had all day.

'It's okay. Zahan isn't a bad guy. He just gets carried away sometimes,' he said.

'I'm Rhea. Rhea Singh,' she said.

'So, Rhea, would you like to have sex on the beach?' Saahil asked Rhea nonchalantly.

Rhea's mouth dropped open, 'I'm sorry, what?'

Saahil hid his grin again. Another one falls for it.

'The cocktail. Sex on the Beach? It has rum in it? Ring any bells?'

There was a sound of a table crashing to the floor. The drunkenness was reaching another level in the apartment.

'Nope. Can't say that I have,' Rhea laughed.

He was making her nervous. Saahil could see it so clearly. He couldn't explain it but he loved the fact that he was having an effect on her.

'Okay, no worries. We'll just stick to tequila then,' he replied. 'So, Rhea, are you new to London?'

'Oh, yes! I just got here, in fact. I'm starting at London College of Fashion tomorrow,' she replied excitedly.

'Oh! LCF! That's a pretty good school, Rhea. I didn't know I was in the company of such brilliance,' Saahil winked at her.

She blushed. 'The goal is to be the next Christianne Mon Fallinger. She's my idol.'

Saahil gave her a questioning look.

'CMF? She's one of the most legendary designers in the world. I would kill for a chance to meet her,' Rhea stated.

Just at that moment, one of his friends' decided to come up to the both of them.

'Saahil, mate! What are you doing over here?' Colin exclaimed. Colin was one of Saahil's closest friends in London.

'Oh, hi. Didn't see the lady back here,' Colin continued when he saw who Saahil was talking to.

He was eyeing Rhea with interest now and Saahil didn't like it one bit.

'Just excuse us for a second, Rhea,' he told her and led Colin away.

'I'll see you later, buddy,' Saahil informed Colin.

Colin held his hands up, 'Hey, man. I just came over to see where you were. She's all yours. So does that mean your blonde friend is available now?' Colin's eyes sparkled.

'Yes. Now, goodbye,' Saahil replied and walked back to Rhea.

'Sorry about that, Rhea,' Saahil said.

'Oh, that's not a problem. So, what about you? Are you a student?' Rhea asked.

'Well, I guess you could say that. I did enrol in the master's in management programme at Regents University. But, my memory is a bit blurry so I could be lying,' he replied.

It was true. He was apparently supposed to be doing his master's in London, but he honestly couldn't remember the last time he'd attended a lecture.

'I'm sorry. I can't tell if you're joking or not,' Rhea said in a shocked voice.

Oh, great. She is one of those serious types.

'Enough about me. Let's talk about something else,' Saahil changed the topic. Discussing academics was his least favourite topic—maybe because he didn't have much to offer on the subject.

'Would you like to sit down?' He asked Rhea.

'Sure,' she smiled.

Saahil guided her to a nearby chair and she made herself comfortable.

'Where are you from, Rhea?' Saahil asked.

Rhea laughed, 'I still get confused by that question. I've lived in Delhi all my life but we moved to Mumbai a year ago. So, I guess the correct answer is Mumbai.'

'Pooja! Stop falling around!' A loud voice rang through the apartment.

The loud proclamation went unnoticed by the entire apartment.

'Oh, wow. I'm from Mumbai as well,' Saahil replied.

They both smiled at each other.

Rhea checked her watch and sighed, 'It's getting so late. I want to wake up early before class tomorrow, but I guess I should wait for Neha.'

No way. She can't be leaving already.

'Oh, you're here with Neha?' Saahil asked. 'Neha Agrawal?'

Rhea's face brightened, 'Yes. You know her?'

'We've met a couple of times socially. She's a nice girl,' Saahil said. 'How do you know her?'

'Oh, Neha and I go way back. We were in school together in Delhi,' Rhea explained. 'Which reminds me…I should really go find her…'

'Relax, Rhea. LCF isn't going to go anywhere. I see that you're still holding on to your shot,' Saahil indicated at her full glass.

'Oh, yeah, I completely forgot about it.'

Saahil poured himself a shot as well and they both downed it.

'God, this is some good tequila,' Rhea said. 'It's so smooth!'

'Which means that we should take another shot.'

'No way. I really can't, Saahil. Have to be up early tomorrow,' she replied. 'Don't you have class in the morning as well?'

Saahil laughed, 'I really have no idea, Rhea.'

'But…aren't you scared? What if you get into trouble?' Rhea asked in a concerned voice.

'Big deal. It's only classes. And as long as I pass the course, it doesn't really matter,' Saahil said casually.

He saw a dawn of realization come upon her face. She now knew that he didn't care about his academics at all—probably because he had some other backup, or he was just an idiot to not care.

'I see,' Rhea commented.

There was an awkward silence as Rhea's demeanour towards Saahil shifted slightly.

Warning. Warning. Saahil's mind was giving off danger signals.

'Anyway. Tell me something else about yourself,' Saahil changed the topic once again.

Just at that moment, Neha re-entered the living room with Pooja.

'Rhea! There you are! I was afraid you might have left already. Oh, hi Saahil. Thanks for keeping Rhea company,' Neha said smilingly.

'Oh, it should be the other way around. I should thank Rhea for keeping *me* company,' Saahil looked at Rhea piercingly.

He saw her expression change again. It really was amazing to see so many expressions on a single face.

Pooja had passed out on the couch by now. Saahil hated such public displays of drunkenness.

'Rhea, we can leave now, if you want,' Neha said to Rhea.

No way! She wasn't going to spoil his evening. He won't let her.

'Guys, come on, stay for a bit. The place is finally clearing out. We can now hear each other at a normal decibel level,' Saahil said.

'Saahil, I should be getting back now. Have an early lecture tomorrow morning,' Neha said.

Saahil saw Rhea get up from her seat and adjust her purse on her shoulder.

He inched closer to her and whispered in her ear, 'So, what do you say we continue this further at my place?'

She looked up at him, confused.

Was this girl really that slow or was she pretending? Whatever it was, Saahil could feel his headache returning.

'Continue what?' She replied.

'You know what I mean. Why don't we let Neha leave and continue our own private party?'

Okay, now he'd blown it. He saw an expression of pure disgust come over her face.

'If we weren't surrounded by so many people, I would have slapped you. I thought you were a guy who was actually interested in conversation, but guess not,' she whispered. 'Now, get away from me, you imbecile!'

Saahil watched Rhea and Neha leave. He was shocked and impressed at the same time.

As soon as they were out of hearing distance, he started to laugh.

That was the most fun he'd had in a while. Rhea's expression when he'd suggested going to his place had almost been comical.

Rhea Singh was certainly an interesting girl.

four

Two Weeks Later

'Your total winds up to…two hundred pounds, sir,' the guy who delivered the food from Hakkasan said.

Saahil reached into his pocket and paid him quickly. He had a special tab with the Michelin star restaurant. There was no way they would deliver food to apartments otherwise.

The Asian food smelt amazing and he couldn't wait to dig in.

'Guys. Food's here,' he announced as he re-entered the living room.

No reply. At any given point of day, he always had at least two–three people taking up space in his apartment. Rather than get annoyed at the fact that he had zero privacy, Saahil loved the intrusion.

It was being alone that actually scared the fuck out of him.

'Zahan! Parth!' Saahil shouted once again.

Once again, there was no reply. They were probably in the game room.

Saahil padded across his three-bedroom Hyde Park apartment toward the game room that he'd had specifically installed. It was the perfect way to unwind after a long day.

A long day of doing what? Drinking copious amounts of alcohol and roaming around endlessly with your entourage?

Saahil ignored that thought. He passed a mirror on the way and caught sight of himself. He really needed to shave.

He opened the door to his game room and saw that Zahan and Parth were engrossed in a game of FIFA. The room consisted of a state-of-the-art television unit that he'd hooked on to all mediums of gaming possible, a pool table that Saahil still had to make use of, and a set of drums. He'd started playing the drums way back when his parents were in the middle of their divorce, and had found that they were incredibly cathartic.

'Guys, come on, I'm starving,' Saahil stated.

'Yeah, sure. Can you just hand me my beer can, Saahil? It really works up my appetite, bro,' Zahan said while staring dead ahead at the screen.

Saahil went up to the television unit and shut off the main power button. 'There. Now you can get it yourself,' he said.

His friends had such an incredulous expression on their faces that he couldn't help laughing, 'Into the living room, boys. I think I've ordered enough for an army.'

There was a sudden ping on his cell phone. It was an e-mail from his Leadership module professor:

```
Please note that the written assignment
spoken about in the lecture will be due three
days from now. Once again, this assignment is
20 per cent of your entire grade, so please
don't take it lightly. You can hand in a
hard copy or e-mail it—up to you. Good luck.
```

Shit. Now Saahil had to find out what this assignment was all about and somehow manage to put down something on paper.

He was supremely fucked.

'What's the matter, Saahil? You look stressed,' Parth commented.

'Hate to break it to you guys, but we have some assignment due in three days. Did you know anything about this?' Saahil asked.

Once again, they had those incredulous expressions on their faces.

'Excuse me? An assignment?' Zahan sputtered.

'Can they just spring it on us like that? We really need a warning on these things,' Parth shook his head.

Okay, his friends and him really needed to get their heads out of their asses. If they weren't so fucked at the moment, Saahil would have most definitely laughed at the situation.

'I'm sure they didn't just spring it on us, Parth. If one of us actually bothered to check the syllabus, I'm sure it'll be on there,' Saahil chuckled.

'True, bro. My father's going to fuck my life if I end up failing this year. His only two conditions were that I don't fail and don't end up in jail,' Parth informed.

Funny. Saahil's father had put down more or less the same conditions. It wouldn't look good on the company newsletter if the boss's son wound up in jail.

'Zahan, why don't we ask that girl you like? She can tell us more about this assignment,' Saahil said.

Zahan blushed a shade of deep red. He was majorly into this girl named Sana in their class. While it was obvious to the rest of the world how much Zahan liked her, she was completely oblivious.

'Yes. I will ask her,' he said.

'Jeez. You're a girl when it comes to her, dude,' Parth said in horror.

Saahil held up a hand. 'I can't get into this now. Please, let's eat. I'm afraid I'm going to pass out from starvation otherwise.'

Just as he was about to scoop some stir-fried vegetables on to his plate, Saahil's phone rang. He saw that it was his mother calling.

'Guys, I'll be back. I need to take this,' he motioned to his phone and went into his bedroom.

'Hi, Mom,' he answered.

'Saahil, hello, my darling son. How are you?' Payal asked.

'I'm fine, Mom, how are you? Is everything okay?' He enquired.

'Of course, it's okay! Can't I just call up my son and ask how he's doing? There doesn't need to be a reason, Saahil,' Payal said with her voice quivering.

Saahil sighed. His mother had drunk called him.

Again.

Her words were slightly slurred, and her emotions jumped up and down every time he spoke to her while she was drunk. He had realized long ago that his mother was a day-drinker as well.

'I'm sorry, Mom. I didn't mean to upset you. Let's talk about something else,' he said patiently. He really didn't want to get into a fight with her.

'Yes, let's discuss something else. When are you coming to see me, beta? I really miss you,' she said sadly.

Do you really miss your son or is it the wine talking?

Instead, Saahil said, 'I miss you too. How are Nana and Nani doing?'

She had moved back to Pune after his grandparents had gone to get her that fateful night. Not that she still lived with them—his grandparents had bought her a separate place. They had found out that their daughter had become extremely bitter post her separation and not a single day passed where they didn't get into a huge fight. This separate living situation was working out well for them—Payal didn't have to live by anyone's rules and all relationships remained cordial.

Little did anyone know that his mother would turn into a raging alcoholic.

'Oh, they're fine. Hold on, Saahil,' Payal said. He could hear her pouring something into a glass.

'You never answered my question, beta. When are you coming home?' She asked again.

'Soon, Mom. A couple of months,' Saahil replied.

'So, are you going to stay with me for even a couple of days or just stay with that father of yours the entire time?' Her voice had a sharp edge to it now.

His parents had decided that it was for the best that Saahil remain with his father post the divorce proceedings. There was no point in uprooting his life as well.

However, the only memory he had of the incident was that they hadn't even bothered asking *him* where he wanted to stay.

Saahil shook his head. There was no point in thinking about all those details.

'I'll definitely try, Mom. I can't say for sure, though. I'm starting work at Dad's office this winter break,' Saahil informed her.

Oops. Saahil realized in the next second that he'd made a blunder of the highest degree. He felt like kicking himself for making such a rookie mistake.

'Excuse me? What do you mean you'll try? Of course, *I'm* the only one you have to try with. When it comes to your father, you're always available! Just cause you live with him doesn't mean you have to be at his beck and call, Saahil! Or is it cause he's the one with the billion dollar company? No, wait, maybe it's due to the fact that he's built you a new mansion on Altamount Road and you can't demean yourself by staying in my apartment! Paying your bills doesn't make him numero uno in your life. Does your mother hold no importance at all? I'm the one who gave birth to you! What did your father do for you? Nothing! I'll tell you what he did—nothing!' Payal screamed over the phone.

Served him right for opening his mouth in the first place.

'Mom,' Saahil said. 'You know I don't care about this new house. I'll always consider the house *we* lived in together close to my heart.'

His father had decided to move Saahil and his grandparents to a new house three years back. The old house had stopped matching his 'status'.

Not that Saahil cared.

Saahil hadn't let his father sell the old house. He still went there to play his *House of the Dead* video game whenever he needed to vent out his frustration.

His mother was still shouting. She obviously hadn't heard what he'd said.

Payal had resorted to crying, 'I love you so much, son. I miss you so much. Don't you know that?'

Saahil shook his head in disgust. He couldn't handle any more of this conversation.

'I'm sorry, Mom. I didn't mean to upset you. Of course, I'll stay with you as well. Whatever you say,' Saahil said in an emotionless voice.

'Oh! That's great, Saahil,' Payal said happily. She was exuberant again. 'I'm so excited! Love you, beta.'

After they had hung up, Saahil just stood on the spot for a couple of minutes. His mind was blank.

This was so typical. He was surprised it still managed to affect him.

He decided to head back outside.

'Saahil! Where did you disappear to, bro? We're almost done with dinner,' Zahan said with his mouth full.

'Oh. That's okay,' Saahil said as he stepped over to the bar in the corner of the living room. 'I think I'm going to have a drink first.'

Maybe have a couple of drinks. And then play the drums.

'Really? I thought you were starving,' Parth commented in a confused tone.

'I was, wasn't I? Well, not anymore,' Saahil said with an edge to his voice.

He brought over the bottle of whiskey to where his friends were sitting and said, 'How about we ask the rest of the crew what they're up to? Let's get wasted tonight.'

'Um…Saahil, what about that assignment you just told us about?' Zahan asked.

'Fuck it. We'll figure it out,' Saahil said.

'Okay. I'll start calling people up. I must say, bro, I love these spontaneous plans of yours!' Zahan exclaimed happily.

'I aim to please,' Saahil said as he downed his drink in a single gulp.

His family would be perfect for a television show. Keeping up with the Kapoors.

There was never a dull moment with the Kapoors.

'Oh, by the way, I forgot to mention it to you, Saahil. Neha is hosting a party at her place next weekend. We should definitely check it out,' Zahan informed.

Saahil's ears perked up.

That meant Ms Rhea Singh was going to be at the party as well.

He had really enjoyed talking to her at Pooja's party.

Before the night progressed and his judgement was clouded by whiskey, his last coherent thought was that things didn't seem so bad anymore.

five

'One hot chocolate to go, please!'

The loud voices of customers were keeping Rhea on her toes. She'd always wondered how people working in coffee joints could move so fast.

Now she knew.

Rhea had decided to take up a part-time job at one of the local coffee places near campus—Cafe Moreno. She'd realized straightaway that living in London was no joke. She needed the extra cash, and she needed it fast.

'John, can you help out with the hot chocolate? I'm still working on the cappuccino!' she exclaimed to the guy working alongside her.

'Sure thing, Rhea.'

Rhea was exhausted. Between her hours at Cafe Moreno and her lectures, there was hardly any time to spare.

Well, there was definitely an upside to the situation. There was no need for her to join a gym—being on her feet all day serving coffee did the job better than any elliptical machine.

'Rachel made it look so damn easy,' she muttered under her breath.

She was obviously referring to Jennifer Aniston's character on *F.R.I.E.N.D.S.*

She served the cappuccino to the lady who had ordered it and realized that she needed to go to the bathroom. 'I'll be right back, John.'

On the way back from the bathroom, her cell phone pinged. It was a message from her mother:

```
Skype later tonight?? Miss you!
```

Rhea smiled and quickly typed out a reply:

```
Definitely! Will call you once I'm back in
my room. In case I don't call till late,
please don't stay up.
```

There was no way she was telling her mother that she was working part-time in the coffee shop. She would flip knowing that Rhea had to work for extra money. Then she would go on to say that she would send Rhea more money and that would lead to a full-blown argument. In order to win the argument, her mother would then bring up her father and how he would have hated the fact that Rhea was working for extra money *along* with studying full-time. And once her father came into the argument, Rhea knew she didn't have a chance of winning against Simran Singh.

Rhea didn't want to stress her out unless it was unavoidable.

She definitely deserved a brownie for being such a considerate daughter.

Another ping.

This time it was from one of her classmates from her Fashion Practice and Critical Contexts module:

```
Hi. Just wondering if you're as lost as
I am in our assigned readings.
```

Okay, this definitely didn't require a reply. Partly because Rhea still hadn't even started her readings. She'd been so caught up with unpacking her suitcases and scoping out the London scene that she'd sort of put studying on the back burner.

Her courses were so freakishly hard that Rhea couldn't think straight. Most of it was also due to the fact that Rhea was used to the Indian system of things, and while there were similarities, the London style of studying was unique in many ways.

The worst part of the system was that there was equal importance placed on the theory of fashion along with the practical aspects of it. Rhea had always had trouble with subjects that were reading-intensive.

Why the fuck was it important what people wore back in the 1700s? And did we really need to know what was happening all the way back in the 1700s?

Someone needed to have a word with the humans who decided the way these courses were structured.

Scholarship, scholarship, scholarship! Rhea reminded herself.

If she didn't get her act together fast, Rhea could kiss her dream of being a fashion designer goodbye faster than the time it took for Britney Spears's wedding to fail.

Her only saving grace was the practical portion of the courses. They had to apply their own individual past knowledge of fabrics and designs and create a specific garment.

When Rhea had heard the description of their tasks, she was dancing internally. Finally, she could use her experience at Kavita Mehta to good use. Make a skirt in three hours? Pfft! She could do it in two. And when it came to creating something unique for the final exam, Rhea already had an idea for the lehenga she could make.

Now all she had to do was find excessive amounts of sequins, rhinestones, a wide array of coloured velvet, and she was done!

'Rhea? Rhea? We're sort of in our peak time, so could you please come back and help?' John asked as he walked up to where Rhea was standing. He had an alarmed look on his face.

'Oh. Shit. Sorry, John. Tell me what orders are up!' Rhea exclaimed as she jolted out of her thoughts.

She'd totally lost track of time and didn't realize how long she'd been transfixed on that spot staring into space.

'Concentrate, you freak,' she muttered to herself. She literally could not afford to mess this up.

By the time Rhea finished her shift, she felt as if she'd run a marathon.

She would never underestimate people who went to the gym ever again. Maybe if she'd ever taken up exercising, she wouldn't feel as if the world was coming to an end.

'See you tomorrow, John! Sorry for leaving you stranded earlier,' Rhea apologized to her colleague. 'I just spaced out.'

'Hey, no stress, Rhea. We all have those days. Say…would you like to go have a slice of pizza or something? I know this really good place downtown,' John asked.

Uh…is he asking me out?

Rhea eyed John objectively for the first time since they'd met a couple days back. He was excessively tall, too thin and wore big glasses on his face—John reminded Rhea of one of her extended relatives back home in India.

Once that comparison had been made, there was no way she could ever think of dating him.

'I'm so sorry John, but I have this really early lecture tomorrow, so I need to get back—' Rhea started.

'Oh, no worries. I get it,' John interrupted awkwardly and

went into the storeroom.

Shit. She should have let him down easy. But what could have been easier than that?

He's certainly not covering for me again. Crap!

As she started walking out towards her accommodation building, Rhea's phone pinged once again. She certainly was popular tonight.

```
Hi.
```

That was all the text said, and since it was an unknown number, Rhea had no idea who it was.

She typed:

```
Who's this?
```

The reply came almost instantly:

```
Saahil.
```

Rhea almost dropped her phone. She definitely hadn't given him her phone number. How the hell was he texting her?

Okay, there was no need to freak out. There had to be a logical explanation for this.

Rhea eyed the text message again, hoping it would give her some clue as to how he had gotten her number.

All of a sudden, her phone started ringing. It was a different number compared to the one she'd received the text message from, but unknown nonetheless.

She decided to let it go to voice mail. If it was Saahil, she hoped that he would get the message and not bother her again.

Oh, fuck! The unknown number was calling her again.

Rhea took a deep breath and murmured to herself, 'Please don't let it be him, please don't let it be him!'

'Hello?' She asked tentatively.

'Rhea! Why the hell aren't you answering your phone, woman?'

Rhea heaved a sigh of relief. It was Neha.

She really needed to start saving numbers on her cell phone.

'Hey. I just got done with my shift at the coffee shop. Sorry, I hadn't saved your number. What's up?' Rhea asked.

'Thanks, dude. I'm the only person you know in London and you don't even save my number. Nice. Anyway, what are you up to? Do you want to hang out? We can order some food,' Neha suggested.

'Sounds good. By the time you get here, I'll be finished with my Skype session with Mom as well, so the timing is perfect. I'm starving,' Rhea said.

She hung up and felt herself relax.

There were no more messages from Saahil. After the tiring day she'd just had, the last thing she wanted to do was talk to a jerk like him.

six

'Rheaa? Rheaaa? Can you see me now, beta?' Simran exclaimed.

Why are mothers so technologically inept?

Once she'd picked up the call, the battle had been explaining to her mother where the video button was.

Rhea sighed into the computer screen, 'Mom. Seriously. Stop it. It's the button that looks like a video camera. You know what that looks like. Bottom left corner!'

'Don't get angry, beta! Oh wait, I see it now,' Simran yelled triumphantly.

After what seemed like endless back and forth, Rhea could finally see her mother on the screen.

'You look so pretty, Rhea! London is definitely suiting you,' Simran said.

'Thanks, Mom, but I look the same as I did when I left India!' Rhea exclaimed.

'Maybe it's the distance. I don't know. But, you're a 100 times prettier now that you're thousands of miles away,' Simran winked.

Rhea laughed, 'Your logic makes so much sense.'

Suddenly, Simran frowned, 'Have you lost weight? Please don't tell me that for the first time in your life, you've started hitting the gym.'

Yes, I have. It's called Cafe Moreno.

'Nope, no gym. It's probably all the walking around that I get to do in London. But, Mom, this place is fantastic! You would love it. I can easily spend an entire day all by myself and not get bored. I'm not joking. There's just so much to do and see. And the food...I don't even know how to describe it. It's better than anything I've ever eaten in the last twenty-three years of my life,' Rhea said excitedly. 'There's this tiny place right next to Selfridges—that's the huge-ass departmental store I was telling you about—and they serve the best spaghetti in the world. The place itself is so simple and tiny that it feels as if you're sitting in one of those roadside cafes in Italy!'

Simran laughed, 'Go on. Tell me more! How's your campus?'

Rhea thought for a moment and continued, 'It's not really a campus, to be honest. They have these buildings scattered across London, so it doesn't have the feel of a proper college. I'm in the building at Marylebone. It's pretty central so I don't have to commute a lot for anything.'

Simran said, 'That's so good, Rhea. Imagine how tired you would have been if you had to walk a lot to get to each and every lecture!'

True. She'd lucked out in that sense.

Simran continued, 'Show me your room. I want to see what you've done with it.'

Rhea gave a short laugh, 'You're going to be very disappointed.'

Rhea turned her laptop around the room so that her mother could get a good view of her humble abode. Yes, that's the feel she was going for—humble.

'Well. It's certainly bare,' Simran said in a deadpan tone.

Rhea almost didn't hear her phone ring due to the loud noise of her laughter.

'Mom, hold on. Neha is here. I have to go let her in the

building,' Rhea said as she dashed off downstairs.

A couple of minutes later, they re-entered her room with the delicious smell of pizza wafting across their senses.

'Hello, Simran aunty! It's been so long since I've seen you! You still look beyond gorgeous,' Neha said as she settled herself comfortably on the bed.

'Hi, Neha! I know, beta. It's been really long. You should definitely come to Mumbai when you guys are back home,' Simran replied.

Rhea tried to get on to the bed as well but was pushed away by Neha. 'Dude. Can't you see it's only big enough for one person? Take the chair,' Neha said.

Gee, thanks, friend.

They rearranged the laptop on the bed so that all three could see each other.

'That pizza looks amazing,' Simran said.

Rhea could see that her mother was almost salivating at the sight of them eating and laughed, 'Mom, I'm sure you have some junk food lying around the apartment. Get it out and eat with us.'

Simran's face brightened, 'Good idea. I think I'll eat my soya sticks.'

Okay, now soya sticks was probably the king of all junk food.

Neha looked at us both in disgust when Simran got back. 'How the hell are both of you so skinny? I would probably weigh a 100 kilograms if I ate the way both of you do. I don't know much about your eating patterns, Simran aunty, but your daughter here is incapable of eating anything healthy!' Neha said.

It was true. Her mother and she survived on eating food

that was most likely really bad for them. Once, they'd tried eating healthy and their bodies had revolted maybe because it was so used to junk being poured into it every single day. This probably wasn't true but it was best to be ignorant sometimes.

Simran knocked on a table next to her and said, 'Touchwood. I hate green vegetables.'

Neha laughed in-between bites and said, 'You're the coolest, Sim Aunty.'

Rhea chimed in, 'So, Mom, what's going on with you?'

Simran replied, 'Oh, nothing really, beta. It's the same usual routine of going to work and coming back and binge watching some television show or the other. Nothing exciting. Oh, wait! I'm thinking of getting a dog.'

Rhea looked at her mother in horror and put her pizza aside. 'But…you hate dogs.'

'No, I don't,' Simran said innocently.

'Yes, you do.'

'No, I don't.'

The same exchange of words would have probably continued for a while had it not been for Neha. 'Relax, guys. You've made your thoughts very clear with the "you do" and "you don't",' she said in an amused tone.

Rhea's phone pinged:

```
Hello?
```

It was Saahil. It was the same number from which he'd messaged her previously.

Rhea tried to keep her face from turning red but couldn't.

'So, guys, let's move to juicier topics,' Neha said with a gleam in her eye. 'Rhea, anything interesting happen today?'

She eyed Rhea's phone.

Oh my God! She was the culprit!

Rhea reached across the distance separating the both of them and slapped Neha's arm. 'I could kill you! Why did you give him my number?'

'Give who your number? Fill me in!' Simran yelled.

'Can we talk about this stuff in front of your mom?' Neha asked hesitantly.

Rhea sighed dejectedly. 'Sure, go ahead.'

'This is so cool, guys! I could never talk about boys in front of my mother!' Neha exclaimed.

'Get to the point, girls!' Simran yelled in frustration.

'So, this friend of mine named Saahil asked for Rhea's number and I gave it to him. I didn't think she would be upset about it. The two of them seemed to have hit it off at the party we went to two weeks ago, anyway,' Neha explained.

'Rhea, why didn't you mention any of this earlier? Tell me more about him! What did you talk about? How is he as a person?' Simran began her endless stream of questions.

Rhea groaned, 'There's nothing to tell. He's a jerk.'

Neha frowned, 'Really? That's not the vibe I got when I saw the two of you talking. Shit. Maybe I was mistaken. If I'd known you didn't have a good time, Rhea, I would have never given him your number. I was pleasantly surprised to get his call today in the first place—there seemed to be some huge party going on wherever he was. There were so many loud voices in the background!'

Rhea hadn't told Neha about the pass Saahil had made at her. She didn't want her friend to be biased against him.

Neha continued, 'I mean, I honestly don't know much about him. He's close to a couple of my friends, which is how I met him in the first place. All I know is that his father owns one of the biggest steel-manufacturing plants in India and, therefore, people really suck up to Saahil. He always has an entourage around him. They all go to that rich, spoilt brat school—Regents. But how he really is as a person—I have no idea.'

'Yes, that's it, Mom. There's nothing more to tell. He just isn't my type of guy,' Rhea said.

But why did he have to be so hot?

Rhea shook her head. There was absolutely no need for such thoughts. She wasn't the sort of person who hooked up randomly with guys and she wasn't going to start now. It may be the new trend, but Rhea couldn't handle casual hook-ups.

Simran seemed disappointed. 'I got excited there for a minute.'

Rhea suddenly remembered John. 'Oh, yes. I did get asked out by this other guy today.'

She told them both about how John had asked her out for pizza. 'But, he resembled Arpit from Delhi, so there was no way I could have gone out with him.'

'Who's Arpit?' Neha asked.

'A cousin from Delhi,' Rhea explained.

'Rhea. You have too many hang-ups. You need to chill,' Neha shook Rhea by her shoulders.

'I am plenty chilled, thank you very much,' Rhea said firmly.

Simran laughed, 'You'll meet someone else. Neha, you need to introduce her to more people. Otherwise, once classes start full-fledged, the only place you see her will be the library.'

Great. They were ganging up against her.

Neha replied, 'Not to fear, aunty. I'm on it. Rhea and I are throwing a party at my place next week.'

They were? Funny how it was the first time Rhea was hearing about it.

Rhea threw up her hands and said, 'Well, there you go, Mom. Guess I'm hosting a party for people I don't even know yet.'

Neha suddenly sighed, 'I really miss Karan sometimes. Especially when I have to throw all these social scenes by myself. Why does he have to be far away? No offence, Rhea.'

None taken, Neha, none taken.

Neha had been dating Karan Malhotra for a little over two years now. Unfortunately, he was in culinary school in Italy, so they didn't get to see each other much.

'Now, who's Karan?' Simran asked. She seemed exasperated with the sudden influx of so many new names.

'My boyfriend, aunty. We've been dating since we were both in Delhi. He goes to school in Italy so we have been in a long-distance relationship for quite some time now,' Neha explained.

Now it was Simran's turn to sigh. 'You girls are so lucky. There's so much excitement in your lives and so much to look forward to. Make the most of it, girls.'

It was time for the conversation to change.

Rhea could see that her mother was getting melancholic. Pretty soon, she was going to start missing her father and Rhea didn't want the conversation to end on a sad note.

'Now, about that dog...' Rhea said.

It was the perfect topic change and pretty soon, the three of them were engrossed in a heated discussion regarding the pros and cons of Simran owning a dog.

Rhea won hands down.

seven

One Week Later

It was Saturday night and Rhea was ready to blow off some steam.

Her workload had been picking up pace, and when she wasn't stressing out about college, she was busy serving coffee at Cafe Moreno.

She walked over to the table where all the alcohol had been placed and started to fix a drink for herself. The party that she and Neha were apparently hosting together was finally here. Rhea had decided to get dressed at Neha's apartment, so she'd arrived way before time.

Looking around the apartment, Rhea observed that her friend had a really nice place. Since Neha had done her undergraduate degree in London as well, she'd found a pretty good place by the time it was time for her masters' programme.

'Hmm. We forgot to put out salt,' Rhea murmured to herself as she looked at the table. She was going to make herself a concoction of soda, lime, salt and vodka.

Basically, a fresh-lime soda mixed with vodka. Most people didn't understand the point of this drink—you didn't really know whether it was going to get you drunk—until it actually did. Rhea loved it.

Heading back to the kitchen to get salt, Rhea smoothed out

the short black dress she'd decided to wear with red pumps. At least this party had given her a chance to dress up. Ever since she'd come to London, there had been absolutely no time to relax and have fun.

'Rhea! Have people started coming?' Neha burst into the kitchen.

'Wow, Neha, you look hot,' Rhea commented. Her friend was dressed in a low cut red dress and had left her long black hair cascading down her back.

Neha brushed the comment away, 'Please. You're one to talk. You could pass off for a model. Now, leave the kitchen and go back out! I'll be out soon.'

Rhea didn't need to be told twice. The kitchen was her least favourite room in any house.

⁂

In the next hour or so, the apartment was filled with people.

Someone had put on music, and it was literally the worst music ever. Deep house. Rhea hated this sort of music. She was all for a good beat, but it needed lyrics.

She was on her third drink by now, and pleasantly buzzed.

'Hey.' Neha materialized by her side. 'Having fun?'

'Yep, can't complain.' Rhea held up her almost empty glass.

Neha laughed, 'Go on and get a refill. I'm going to take you around the room to introduce you to people then.'

Rhea walked over to the table once again and was in the process of making her drink, when someone tapped her shoulder. 'Funny how we keep meeting next to the bar.'

It was complete déjà vu. Rhea didn't need to turn around to know whose voice it was.

However, she had forgotten just *how* good looking Saahil

really was. He was dressed head to toe in black. According to Rhea, head to toe in black was the biggest faux pas anyone could make, but Saahil somehow carried it off.

Rhea shook her head. Her brain somehow always turned to mush around him.

She gave him a cold stare. 'I'm sorry, I'm blocking your way. Please feel free to make yourself whatever it is that you're having.'

She was about to walk away when Saahil reached out and lightly touched her arm. 'Can I just talk to you for a minute, Rhea? I want to apologize for what happened the last time we met. Please, hear me out for a minute. Please.'

Rhea searched his face for a sign that he was lying in any way, but he looked sincere.

Maybe it was the vodka that clouded her judgement, but Rhea decided to stay and listen to what he had to say.

'Fine. You have a minute,' she said. 'Oh, wait. I need to make my drink first.'

'Let me do that for you,' Saahil said. He quickly made her drink as per her specifications and made himself a whiskey on the rocks.

'Okay. Go on,' Rhea said.

'I'm really sorry for the way I acted that day, Rhea. I don't know what came over me. First off, I'm a really dumb guy. Like, really dumb. I do stuff without thinking of the consequences, and that's my biggest flaw,' Saahil began. He held up a hand when he saw that Rhea was about to speak and continued, 'I know this isn't an excuse for my behaviour. I was enjoying our conversation so much before I messed up. I shouldn't have said what I did. It was after I actually said those things that I realized what a fucking idiot I am. I won't lie to you, Rhea—I think you're really pretty. I just acted on impulse that day. I just...I don't know what I'm trying to say. I tried to message you so that I could apologize sooner but I guess you didn't want to hear from me. So...yes. That's all I had to say.'

Damn. That was good.

Rhea just stood for a minute and let his words soak in. He really did look sincere.

'Well? Are you going to say something or should I just walk away?' Saahil asked hesitantly.

Maybe it was the fact that she was really tired or the fact that she was so far away from home, Rhea decided to forgive him. If there one thing she did believe in, it was second chances.

'It's okay. You're forgiven,' she said with a half-smile.

A smile broke out on Saahil's face. 'Great.'

They stood silently next to each other for a moment till someone tapped Saahil on his shoulder. 'Hey, man. Do you have some stuff with you?'

Stuff? What stuff?

'Rhea, this is Parth,' Saahil introduced her to his friend. He took out a small Ziploc bag filled with weed from his pocket and handed it to Parth. 'Who wants it?'

'A bunch of us are smoking right there,' Parth said, pointing to a corner of the house. 'Want to join?'

Saahil looked questioningly at Rhea. She quickly shook her head no.

Wait, maybe...

She waited for Parth to walk away. 'Actually, I don't mind smoking some of that. There's always a first time, right?'

Saahil looked surprised. 'Oh, you mean you've never smoked pot before? Well, I don't know, Rhea. I've just gotten back in your good books—I don't want to be held responsible if you don't enjoy it.'

Rhea quickly downed her drink and said, 'Oh, come on. It's not like I've never smoked a cigarette before. I want to try it!'

'I don't know, man—'

'Oh, come on, Saahil!' Rhea exclaimed.

He looked at her again and asked, 'Are you sure?'

'Yes, I'm sure. Now, go get the stuff before I start questioning myself!' Rhea said firmly.

Saahil smiled, 'Okay. But, I don't want to make you smoke here. Your first time smoking weed should be in a mellow atmosphere. Let's go to Neha's room.'

Rhea's expression must have given away something because he threw up his hands and laughed, 'I swear to you, no funny business. My hands will only be to myself. Even though you look undeniably hot tonight.'

Rhea blushed. *What a smooth talker.*

She watched him walk over to the stoner corner and get some stuff from one of his friends. He motioned her over with his glass still in his hands. 'Lead the way, ma'am.'

Rhea quickly guided him to Neha's room and shut the door slightly. She was excited to get high for the first time.

'Now, just sit, and relax. Wait, put on some music. Something you enjoy,' Saahil instructed.

While she rummaged through Neha's music collection on her laptop, Rhea saw Saahil get to work on rolling the perfect joint. She finally compiled a list of songs on a playlist and played John Legend's *All of Me*.

Saahil smiled while still rolling the joint, 'I love this song.' He drank his whiskey in a single gulp and set the glass aside.

Good taste in music as well...

'Okay. All done,' he announced.

They settled themselves comfortably on the bed, and Rhea watched Saahil as he lit the joint. 'Now all you have to do is inhale, hold for a couple of seconds, and exhale. Yes, just like a cigarette,' he said when he noticed her 'Duh' expression.

He took the first drag and passed it on to her. Rhea took a huge drag and coughed.

'Easy, tiger,' Saahil laughed.

'Nothing happened,' Rhea said.

'Well, you have to wait a couple of minutes. It's not one of those instant things, you know,' he grinned.

Why hadn't she noticed earlier that his eyes sparkled when he smiled? Saahil looked incredibly relaxed as he lounged on Neha's bed and took a drag from the joint.

The playlist moved on to *Of the Night* by Bastille.

Rhea took two huge puffs from the joint when it was passed to her and coughed again. *Why wasn't anything happening? This weed thing is way overrated.*

'I really don't get what the big deal is!' She exclaimed. 'It seems pretty normal to me.'

'Just wait for a few minutes. You're really impatient, you know that?' Saahil said to her.

They passed the joint around for a couple of minutes in relaxed silence. Both of them seemed to enjoy the silence and the mellow music.

Rhea finally felt herself unwind.

She looked around Neha's room and noticed that there were a huge number of books on her table. 'She really has a lot of books for someone who doesn't like to read,' she commented to Saahil.

Saahil looked questioningly at Rhea.

'What?' She asked him.

'Nothing,' he said quickly.

She let her eyes roam around the room again till they got fixated on the white lamp that Neha had on her table.

Fuck!

'Oh my God, Dumbledore's going to kill me with that Deluminator!'

∞

'Rhea. Rhea.'

Someone was shaking her.

Go away. Whoever it is.

'Rhea, wake up. We've reached your building.'

Rhea finally lifted her head from someone's shoulder and opened her eyes to Saahil's amused expression. 'Well, hello, Ms "This Stuff Doesn't Work",' he said.

He was really close to her. Rhea noticed that his eyes were a shade of deep brown.

She finally straightened in her seat and asked, 'What the hell happened?'

'You got really high along with being marginally tipsy, that's what happened. I had to take you away from that loud party before you got even more paranoid,' Saahil explained. 'You should probably let Neha know that you're back home safe. We didn't get time to say goodbye to her.'

Rhea was still having a hard time following his words. *Whatever.* She would deal with it tomorrow.

She tried to get up from the car seat and groaned, 'My legs feel so heavy. How do you know where I live?'

Saahil looked amused again. 'You told me. When we got into the taxi. Your words were pretty hard to understand, but

I managed. Don't worry, I'll help you out.'

Saahil opened the passenger door and helped her out of her seat. He quickly paid the taxi driver before he got annoyed.

With one arm around her waist, he managed to take Rhea up to her room.

She had a hard time opening the door, till Saahil finally took the keys from her hand and opened it.

She was so going to regret this in the morning.

'There. You're back home,' he said triumphantly as they entered the room.

Rhea groaned again. She felt like death.

'Saahil, I want you to know that I'm usually pretty civilized. Now, I just have one last thing to ask of you. Do you like pizza? I swear I could eat an entire one by myself right now.'

Saahil continued to laugh till she decided to ignore him and call Domino's.

Laughter could wait. Cheese could not.

eight

Saahil woke up with a start.

He checked his phone and saw that it was 2.00 p.m.

Fuck. Thank God it was Sunday or he would have missed college yet again.

Saahil coughed violently. The joint last night had screwed up his throat royally. He drank an entire glass of water to clear the scratchiness.

He smiled when he recalled the events of the previous night.

Rhea Singh was an absolute riot to be around.

Of course, it didn't hurt that she looked like a million bucks. When Saahil had helped her get back to her room, he'd noticed that she was extremely tiny. The feel of her waist under his arm had been a clear indication of that.

He walked over to his bathroom and checked his reflection.

'Shit,' Saahil muttered under his breath. His eyes were bloodshot.

For the longest time now, he'd been having trouble sleeping. When he did fall asleep late into the wee hours of the morning, he was incredibly groggy even after waking up. Saahil hadn't experienced a restful night's sleep in a very long time.

He checked his phone again and saw that there was a message from Rhea:

Ummm...

Saahil chuckled. She was probably regretting that joint right about now.

Rhea had taken two bites of the pizza before she passed out. Saahil had left her room with her being absolutely dead to the world.

Before he could type out a reply, his phone rang. It was his father.

Saahil cleared his throat once again before answering. He didn't want his father to know that he'd just woken up.

'Saahil,' Manan said in his usual form of greeting.

'Hi, Dad. What's up?' Saahil replied.

'I'm in London. Had a couple of meetings to attend. What is your plan for the day?' Manan asked.

Shit. Saahil never looked forward to his father's surprise visits.

'Uh…nothing. You tell me,' Saahil said.

'I'll come by your apartment in the next forty-five minutes. It should give you enough time to clear out all the drugs and alcohol that's lying around the living room,' Manan said and hung up.

Saahil wasn't sure but he could have sworn that he heard his father chuckle before putting down the phone.

⁂

'Saahil. Son. Hi,' Manan said as Saahil opened the door.

Manan was dressed in a three-piece suit that emphasized his corporate stature. Recently, he had gotten obsessed with eating right and exercising, and the results were evident. The years of heavy drinking that had started to show on his body seemed to have washed away.

'Hi, Dad. You look great,' Saahil replied.

They stood awkwardly in the doorway for a couple of seconds till Saahil reached out and gave his father a side hug.

Saahil may have lived with his father post the divorce, but they'd never been able to forge a close relationship. Manan had always remained stoic and awkward around him, and as a kid, it hadn't taken Saahil long to pick up on it.

The distance between them had been growing for so many years that it seemed pointless to do anything about it now.

'What would you like to have?' Saahil asked as they walked into the apartment.

'Nothing. I'm good. I just came by to check on you,' Manan replied.

Oh. That was strange. His father had never randomly come by to check up on him.

Over the years, Saahil had somehow managed to bring himself up without any sort of adult supervision. Sure, his grandparents had constantly tried to tend to him, but he'd somehow detached himself from all of them.

'Okay...' Saahil replied with a quizzical look on his face.

'What's wrong? You seem confused,' Manan commented.

'No, nothing,' Saahil said.

They settled themselves on the living room couch and waited for someone to initiate conversation.

Tick-tock. Birds chirping. All the mundane sounds that go by unnoticed in everyday life were all amply clear to Saahil at the moment.

'So...how's college going?' Manan asked finally.

'Good. It's going good,' Saahil replied. 'I have exams soon, before I come back to India in December.'

'And are you still onboard with the plan we discussed

before you came to London? You joining office this winter break?' Manan asked.

So he still remembered. Saahil had half expected his father to forget that they'd ever had such a discussion.

'Yes, we're still on for that,' Saahil said.

Something fishy was going on. His father was never so attentive.

'How are you doing on money? You have enough, right? I can have the office transfer you more money, if you want,' Manan said.

Okay, something was definitely going on now. More money?

Saahil had yet to have a conversation regarding money with his father. He didn't even need to bring up the topic. Saahil just had to speak with his company's business manager and it would always be done.

'I have money, Dad. Don't worry,' Saahil replied. 'How are Dada and Dadi doing?'

'They're fine. Your grandmother really misses you,' Manan said with a smile.

'I'll call her soon,' Saahil commented. He realized that he'd not spoken to his grandparents since he'd come to London.

Not cool.

'And...how's your mother? Doing good?' Manan asked hesitantly.

'Yes, she seems to be doing fine. Okay, Dad, what's going on?' Saahil asked abruptly. 'I know there's a specific reason why you came over today so just tell me what it is.'

Manan sighed, 'Saahil. Listen to me. There's something I need to tell you.'

Yeah, no shit, genius.

'I know we've not been close in the past, and I would like

to change that. You're my only son and I don't want us to be so distant with each other,' Manan said in a hurry.

Huh? Saahil had not seen that coming.

'Um. Okay. Yeah,' he replied.

Manan smiled in relief, 'Okay. Great. Now, there's something else that I need to share with you.'

Here it comes.

'Saahil…I've met someone. It's becoming serious, so I thought I should introduce the two of you. She's waiting outside and would love to meet you,' Manan announced.

Saahil felt his mind go blank. He had no idea what to think.

'Her name is Nandini and she's from Mumbai as well. She's really nice, Saahil. I would love it if the two of you got along,' Manan continued.

'You said she's right outside?' Saahil managed to say.

'Yes! I got her along so that the two of you could meet. She specifically instructed me to make sure that she met you this time. She's wanted to meet you for a while now, Saahil, but I always put it off because I had no idea what you would think. But…I think it's time you met,' Manan said.

Saahil got up and started pacing across the room. His mind was still blank.

Has he completely lost it?

There was such an overflow of emotions inside him that his brain was having difficulty in processing all the information. *How could he do this to me?*

'What about my mother?' Saahil asked finally.

'Saahil. You know your mother and I are divorced. It's been so long, son,' Manan said in anguish.

'Dad…you need to leave,' Saahil said with no emotion in his voice.

Thank God. He was finally in control of what he wanted to portray to his father.

'Saahil, come on. Just meet her. You'll love her,' Manan said in urgency. He'd gotten up from his seat as well.

'Nope. I don't think I will,' Saahil commented.

'Saahil, you're being unreasonable. You know your mother and I aren't together. Haven't been for years and years now,' Manan said.

His expression was of pure shock and worry now.

'Yes, I know that. I'm not psychotic. I know the reality,' Saahil said harshly.

Manan walked to the door. 'Saahil, just meet her—if you have even an ounce of affection for me. You'll know how great she is once you meet her,' he pleaded.

Saahil shook his head no.

Manan opened the door, 'Nandini! Come in!'

What the fuck?

An elegantly dressed woman in her late thirties came to the doorway and smiled. She was extremely pretty and poised.

No wonder he's fallen for her. Tramp.

He saw his father look lovingly at Nandini and almost threw up.

That's it. He couldn't do it anymore.

'Both of you get out! I can't deal with this right now. Leave my fucking apartment right now!' Saahil shouted.

He caught a sight of Nandini's expression. It had changed from happiness to extreme shock and hurt.

'Saahil! Apologize right now!' Manan roared.

'Or what? Are you going to hit me as well?'

There. He'd given his father the ultimate blow. He had no comeback after this.

'Let's go, Nandini,' Manan said quietly.

Saahil watched them leave from the open doorway and realized that there were tears in his eyes.

He went ahead to shut the door when he realized that the corridor still wasn't empty.

Rhea was standing a couple of feet away from his apartment.

nine

'What are you doing here?' Saahil asked a clearly shaken Rhea.

'I-I'm sorry. You didn't reply back so I thought I'd just come see you in person. I-I should go,' Rhea replied.

'No. No. Come in,' Saahil stated.

'Saahil, are you sure? I can just come by later,' Rhea suggested.

No. He needed the distraction.

'Come in, Rhea. I'll just be a second,' he said.

Leaving her standing in the living room, Saahil went to his bathroom to wash up.

He still couldn't wrap his head around what had just happened.

His father had some gall showing up with his girlfriend like that. What did he expect out of Saahil? That he would be happy to see his father with some woman other than his mother?

There was a nagging thought at the back of his head saying that he needed to give this some more time and thought, but currently, all he could think of was punching something.

Fuck. His reflection in the bathroom mirror showed that his eyes were bloodshot once again. But this time, the reason was entirely different.

Rhea couldn't see him in this state. No way. Saahil hid all his demons away from every single person. No one was allowed inside.

Walking back outside, Saahil picked up a whiskey bottle from the bar.

'Sorry about that, Rhea. You walked right into the Kapoor drama. We're pretty well known for that,' Saahil joked.

Was it a joke?

Maybe, maybe not.

Rhea jumped slightly when she heard him. 'Saahil, I really should go. I've caught you at a bad time. I just came by to apologize in person.'

'Apologize? For what?' Saahil asked.

Saahil got out a glass and ice and proceeded to make his trademark whiskey drink.

'Last night? I was the biggest idiot on the planet? Remember that?' Rhea asked.

Saahil laughed, 'You're kidding, right? You were so cute.'

He was forgetting his family drama already. Rhea had been the perfect example of a hot mess last night. Come to think of it, she looked pretty hot even now. Her white turtleneck sweater and black pants hugged her body like second skin, and complemented her frame perfectly.

A confused look came over her face, 'Are you sure? I've been feeling terrible about it all day. I completely spoilt your night as well.'

As far as Saahil could remember, none of his friends had ever apologized to him in case he'd had to take care of them after a crazy night.

'Rhea. Trust me. You didn't spoil my night. In fact, I was highly entertained,' Saahil grinned. 'You told me all about your fantasies and all your fetishes…I certainly hadn't taken you for a whips and chains kind of girl, though.'

'Wh-What? I said that?' Rhea sputtered.

She was so adorable.

'I'm kidding. You said nothing of the sort. I'm just messing with you,' Saahil grinned again. 'Do you want me to make you a drink as well?'

'No. I'm good, thanks,' Rhea answered. She seemed relieved that she hadn't revealed any hidden dark secrets.

Saahil settled down on the couch next to her and sipped his drink. It felt funny to think that just a couple of minutes earlier, it had been his father on the couch, and he'd felt like killing someone.

Now, looking at Rhea, he felt normal again.

She was strumming her fingers and looking straight ahead. Saahil knew that he'd have to broach the topic at some point.

'So. Once again, sorry that you had to witness that earlier,' he started.

'I take it that was your father,' Rhea said tentatively.

'Yep. That's him,' Saahil stated with an edge to his voice.

'And that woman with him was his girlfriend?' She asked.

'Yes,' Saahil replied.

'If you don't mind me asking… Where's your mother?' Rhea asked. 'If you think I'm overstepping, I'll shut up. I promise.'

'No, it's okay. I don't mind discussing it,' Saahil replied.

It was weird but he didn't mind discussing his fucked up family dynamics with Rhea. He felt comfortable around her.

'Mom lives in Pune. She's originally from Pune, so she moved back there once my parents got separated,' Saahil said.

'How long has it been since they got…?' Rhea started hesitantly.

Saahil gave a short laugh, 'It's okay, Rhea. You can mention the "D" word. It's been around nine years since they got officially divorced, and it's been almost eleven years since they first separated.'

'I can't even begin to imagine what you must have gone through, Saahil. I'm sorry,' Rhea said quietly.

Saahil looked at her and sensed something between them. He couldn't pinpoint what it was, but it was definitely something.

'Don't be sorry. There's nothing to be sorry for, Rhea. It's all been forgotten,' Saahil stated.

Only, it wasn't forgotten when his parents dropped bombshells like the one his father just had.

'You must have been what? Eleven? Twelve? That's tough on any kid,' she said.

'It's fine. I just wish some things had turned out differently,' Saahil shared.

'Like what?'

'Well, for starters, I wish I saw Mom more. It's partly my fault that I don't go to Pune more when I know that I should. I just get into a bubble of sorts and it's difficult to pull myself out of it. It's no excuse, but yes, it happens,' Saahil described. 'Oh, you would love meeting my mother, since you're into fashion. Back when she and Dad were married, she used to have her clothing boutique in Mumbai. Running her business was such a huge part of who she was as a person. Of course, when she moved to Pune, all of that went down the drain.'

'Wow, that must have been amazing. I would love to meet her someday and get pointers,' Rhea smiled.

He was starting to feel a little uncomfortable with the road down memory lane and the amount of sympathy she was showering him with.

Plus, he'd shared enough. It was time to change the subject.

'Enough about me. Tell me about yourself,' Saahil asked.

'Well, there's not much to tell. It's just my mother and I. We used to live in New Delhi, but ever since my father passed away a couple years ago, we knew we had to move. That place had too many memories associated with him. I remember that I couldn't pass by a single restaurant without thinking that Dad would have loved eating here. And then I would remember that he's no longer with us. Eventually, it got too much and we decided to move,' Rhea described.

Oh, fuck.

'Shit. I'm so sorry, Rhea. I had no absolutely no idea. You must think I'm an absolute asshole, right? Crying about my parents' problems, when you're the one who had to deal with real loss. I don't know what to say,' Saahil said.

He felt so dumb and tiny compared to the strong woman sitting in front of him. At least he had a father.

'Oh, stop it. Everyone has to deal with some issue or other, Saahil. I'm sure yours was even tougher to deal with in some ways. Both of your parents being there but not being there at the same time. Dealing with it must have been incredibly hard,' Rhea said.

'I don't know. I still feel like a jerk,' he said. 'Anyway. We need to lighten the subject. Are you hungry? I know you didn't get to eat much last night!'

That got a laugh out of Rhea. 'Oh my God, it was so terrible! I was so paranoid and disturbed by that joint! I kept imagining that I'm on a ship and that my ship is going to be hijacked by pirates!'

Saahil laughed, 'And to think you thought that it wasn't working. But, it's surprising you had such a bad reaction to it. I personally love smoking up. Completely de-stresses me.'

'Yeah, well, maybe it was because I've been so stressed about doing well on all my assignments. Since I'm on full scholarship, I have to maintain my grades. Otherwise, I'm totally fucked,' Rhea declared.

Wow. She was smarter than most people if she was in LCF on scholarship.

'Okay, you're making me feel dumber and dumber by the minute. Anyway, back to the original question, are you hungry?' Saahil enquired.

'Well, now that you mention it, I wouldn't mind eating something. Any suggestions?' Rhea asked smilingly.

Saahil's face brightened, 'I was hoping you would say that. Please say you like Italian food.'

Rhea laughed, 'I love Italian food.'

'Great. You're in for a treat then,' Saahil stated.

He took out his phone and dialled a number, 'Hi, Bocca di Lupo? This is Saahil. I'd like a delivery of my usual.'

He spoke for a couple more seconds and hung up. 'It should be here soon. Would you like a tour of the place? I have a sick game room.'

'Sure. Lead the way!' Rhea exclaimed.

Saahil looked at her suddenly and confessed, 'Rhea. Thanks for today. You being here really took my mind off things. In fact, I just had one drink. If I'd been alone after the scene you witnessed, I was seriously in danger of drinking the entire bottle.'

'Glad I could be of assistance,' Rhea smiled at him.

He loved her smile. It made him want to smile himself.

'Can I just ask you one thing?' Saahil questioned.

'Sure. Go ahead.'

'What the hell is a Deluminator?'

ten

Two Months Later

Rhea inched closer to Saahil till their lips met. He was the most amazing kisser. The way his lips moved over hers made her forget about everything in the world except the fact that he was kissing her.

Rhea moaned. She wanted more.

'Move lower, please...' She whispered in between kisses.

'It'll be my pleasure,' Saahil whispered back.

Rhea woke up with a start. Her phone was ringing.

Another dream.

She groaned into her pillow. This had been the third dream in a week's time.

Rhea saw that it was Neha calling and picked up, 'Morning, Neha.'

'Don't you "Morning, Neha" me! Where the fuck have you been?' Neha screamed into the phone.

It was too early in the day to be screamed at. 'How are you up so early? It's so cold. Don't you like sleeping in?' Rhea asked.

It was already December and it was the chilliest winter that Rhea had ever experienced, which also meant that her inner sloth was making an appearance.

'Don't you dare dodge my question. Get ready. I'm coming to pick you up in an hour. We're going to Hyde Park. And it's

Saturday so you don't get to make up excuses about college!' Neha shouted again and hung up.

Hyde Park. That only meant that she was going to be extremely near Saahil's apartment.

His lips sprang to her mind once again and Rhea groaned.

Her mind was really in the gutter these days.

It had been two months since Rhea had witnessed the horrible scene between Saahil and his father. That day, she'd ended up staying for dinner *and* had watched a movie with him.

They'd met each other almost every single day since then.

It had been completely platonic, of course.

Saahil had been the perfect gentleman.

In fact, in the last two months, Rhea had noticed some slight changes within him. He wasn't drinking as much, and he'd started attending his lectures more.

The days when she was laden with work for college, he would sit next to her and do his own assignments, or just read.

She'd discovered that he was an avid reader. Hemingway was his personal favourite. When she'd questioned Saahil about it, he'd confessed that he loved to read. However, the company he surrounded himself with didn't give him a chance to exploit his hobby, so he rarely displayed it.

They had fallen into a pattern. Saahil would call her as soon as he woke up, and they would make plans for later in the day. Rhea had spent more time chilling in his apartment than she had in her own room.

Not that she was complaining about that.

Rhea groaned again and dragged herself out of bed. Neha was definitely going to give her the third degree today. Ever since she'd started spending time with Saahil, she hadn't gotten the time to hang out with Neha. Between lectures, her job at Cafe Moreno and Saahil, Rhea was thoroughly swamped. Not to mention Skyping with her mother. There was no escaping that.

As she was getting dressed, her phone rang again.

Rhea's heart skipped a beat. She knew it was Saahil.

'Hello?' She answered.

'Hi,' Saahil replied. His voice sounded heavy with sleep and made Rhea want to snuggle in bed next to him.

Rhea shook her head. *What is wrong with me?*

'What are you doing?' He enquired.

'I'm going to Hyde Park with Neha. She wants to chill,' Rhea replied.

'Oh. Okay. Come over once you're done? The park is literally two minutes from the apartment,' Saahil explained.

'Alright. I'll do that,' Rhea smiled and hung up.

There was no doubt in her mind that she had started to like Saahil. A lot.

But she had no idea what to do about it. Or *whether* she should do something about it.

∽∞∽

'So. Care to explain yourself?' Neha asked with a frown.

No. No, she didn't.

Rhea and Neha had spread a rug out on the grass, and were sipping on cheap champagne. The warm sun beat down on them and it felt amazing. While the wind around them was extremely chilly, the sun sort of balanced the atmosphere.

Rhea sighed, 'I'm sorry, Neha. There are no excuses.'

'Don't think that I don't know that you've been spending all your time with Saahil,' Neha said.

Rhea looked at her in surprise.

'Yes, that's right. I have eyes and ears everywhere,' Neha said solemnly.

Rhea laughed. Her friend looked extremely proud of the fact that she'd managed to keep track of all of Rhea's activities.

'Guilty as charged,' Rhea confessed.

'How come, though? I thought you hated him,' Neha pointed out.

'True. But…he's not as bad as I thought he was. We just hung out one day and I realized that he's not a bad guy,' Rhea explained.

Saahil certainly had wormed his way in.

'Good. Now that we've brought it out, give me all the scoop,' Neha said excitedly.

Rhea took a sip of her champagne before answering, 'There's not much to tell, honestly. We're just hanging out.'

'Just hanging out. With Saahil,' Neha repeated.

'Yes. Just hanging out,' Rhea said again.

'That is so weird,' Neha said in awe.

'Why? What's so weird about that?' Rhea enquired.

Neha took a minute before answering, 'Well. From whatever I've heard about him, Saahil's not the type of guy who just likes to hang out with girls. He's quite the player. Apparently, he's had more one night stands than the rest of his boy crew combined.'

Ah. That's interesting.

'I had no idea,' Rhea said.

'How would you have any idea? If you had continued to hang out with your friend, you would have heard about it sooner!' Neha shouted.

Enough with the shouting, man.

'So, has he had a lot of relationships as well?' Rhea asked. She wanted to know more about Saahil's sordid love life.

'I don't think so. He's more into flings, I think,' Neha commented.

Rhea was having a hard time believing all these facts. Since the past two months, she hadn't witnessed anything that would confirm Neha's statements.

Saahil had been the complete opposite of a bona fide Casanova.

Now, what he did *after* she went back to her dorm, Rhea had no clue whatsoever.

She suddenly remembered that when they'd first met, he'd tried to hook up with her as well.

It was funny how much she'd despised him after that incident, and now she couldn't stop thinking about kissing him.

'Rhea? What's wrong? Why are you frowning?' Neha asked suddenly.

Rhea jolted out of her reverie. 'Nothing. Just thinking,' she replied.

'I'm sorry. I shouldn't have told you all this. I just wanted you to be careful, that's all. If you ever start liking him, at least you should know all the facts beforehand,' Neha replied.

Too late for that, my friend.

Rhea was already in too deep.

Rhea forced herself to laugh, 'You're right. Anyway. That's enough about my potential love life. I'm just excited to go back home to India once winter break starts.'

∞

Rhea pressed Saahil's doorbell and waited for him to open the door.

Her mind was made up. She knew exactly what she was going to do.

Neha's words had made her realize that if she didn't do something about the situation, she was going to make a fool of herself sooner rather than later.

Saahil opened the door almost instantly and smiled down at her. He had a good couple of inches on her, putting Rhea right at his shoulder level.

Saahil was dressed in a pair of white denim jeans and a baby pink t-shirt. He looked so good that all Rhea wanted to do was grab his head and kiss him.

No. No more kissing thoughts.

'Rhea?' Saahil asked with a questioning look on his face.

Rhea realized that she'd just been standing in his doorway, not saying a single thing.

She chuckled nervously, 'Sorry. Had a little too much champagne.'

At least the champagne had given her the courage to come and talk to Saahil.

'Well, come on in,' Saahil smiled warmly at her. 'I was just in the middle of playing a drum set. Do you mind if I play a couple more minutes?'

'Sure. Go ahead,' Rhea replied.

They entered his game room and Rhea sat down on one of the chairs facing Saahil.

This was the first time she was watching him play the drums. Saahil looked every bit the hot musician.

Her mind went into overdrive, and, once again, all she could think about was how his lips would feel against her skin.

'Rhea? Are you okay?' Saahil enquired, his brow furrowed.

'Huh?' Rhea jolted out of her reverie.

'You have this funny look on your face,' Saahil frowned.
'I'm fine. Go on, play.' Rhea forced herself to smile.
God. This really was a conundrum.
Why did she have to go and start liking him?
Especially when they were so ill-suited for each other.
Rhea let out a huge sigh of frustration.

'Okay, enough. I can't handle it, Rhea. What's on your mind?' Saahil asked abruptly. He put down his drum sticks and came close to her.

He was really good at that. Knowing exactly when someone had a particular thing on their mind and needed to talk about it.

In this situation, though, she had also made it amply clear that something was definitely on her mind.

Rhea started pacing across his game room. 'I can't do this anymore,' she said suddenly.

A confused look came over Saahil's face, 'Do what?'

'This. Us. Hanging out,' Rhea exclaimed.

Rhea wondered for a split second if she was being too impulsive about this, but then shook her head.

Once something had entered her mind that she felt strongly about—it had to be said out loud. It had landed her in trouble more times than she could fathom.

'What? Why not, Rhea?' Saahil asked. He looked shocked. 'Did I do something wrong?'

'No. You didn't do anything. I just…can't hang out with you anymore,' Rhea said quietly.

'Well, why the hell not? You have to give me a logical reason for this, Rhea. You can't just say all these things without a proper explanation!' Saahil exclaimed.

His voice was gaining volume, which meant that he was angry.

'I should go,' Rhea stated softly.

'What do you mean, go? You can't just leave!' Saahil shouted.

Okay, he was really mad now.

Rhea finally stopped pacing and sighed, 'I'm making you angry. I don't want that.'

Saahil looked panicked now. He came slightly closer to where she was standing and softened his voice, 'Rhea. Tell me what's wrong.'

It was her turn to get angry now.

'I can't do this anymore, Saahil! Can't you see that I've started to like you? I can't be around you all the time and just be your friend anymore. I just can't. It's becoming really hard for me now,' Rhea started.

Now that she'd begun talking, she couldn't stop.

'I know you're not the relationship kind. You're into casual flings. Well, I'm not like you, Saahil. I've always been a committed relationship type of girl and I can't change that about myself. So, it's best that we stop hanging out so much,' Rhea said in a rush.

Saahil looked like a truck had hit him. He looked *that* shocked.

Rhea almost wanted to laugh looking at his expression.

'You know I'm not boyfriend material, right?' he finally spoke.

'Yes, I know that. Which is why we should put an end to this,' Rhea said quietly.

She wanted to howl.

'You'd hate me in a relationship, Rhea. Why do you think I don't date anyone? I don't trust myself to be a nice guy. Hell, I don't know what being a "nice guy" even means!' Saahil exclaimed.

'Yes. I don't want to hate you,' Rhea said.

'But, you can't just come in here and say such crap, Rhea!' Saahil shouted.

Crap? Her saying she liked him was crap?

'What do you mean "crap"? I'm letting you off the hook! I don't want anything from you!' Rhea exclaimed.

'Yeah, well, not seeing each other is absolute crap! And I can't deal with that. I can't let go of you. I'm crazy about you. If you haven't noticed, you're the only person I'm interested in spending my time with. All the girls earlier were just a distraction from my own thoughts, Rhea. Now that I've met you…I know what I fool I was,' Saahil shook his head.

Rhea shook her head as well, 'Saahil. You just said that you're not boyfriend material. There's nothing more to say. There's no point to any of this.'

She looked up at him and saw that his eyes were gleaming.

'We're going to give this a shot. You and I. I'm going to be your boyfriend and there's nothing you can do to stop it. I can learn how to be a committed boyfriend,' Saahil said with a slight shudder. 'If that's what will make you happy, then that's what we'll do.'

'You just shuddered at the thought of being a committed boyfriend,' Rhea frowned. 'Rhea. Listen to me,' Saahil said frantically. 'Yes, I'm scared at the thought of being your boyfriend. I'm scared of hurting you. I'm scared because this time it actually means something and I don't want to do anything to fuck it up. Given my track record, the chances of me fucking this up are high, but one thing I know is that I can't let you go. The thought of not being able to see you every day or talk to you every day…that's even scarier.'

Rhea looked up into his eyes and felt herself melt.

She was his for the taking and she knew it.

'You think you're the only one with feelings?' Saahil's voice rose. It was his turn to pace across the room now. 'Well, you're not! I've had a thing for you for a while now, Rhea. Do you know how hard it's been keeping my hands off you? And I was too scared to make a move, thanks to the first time we met.'

Rhea smiled and started walking toward him.

'God. You confuse the hell out of me,' Saahil shook his head again.

Rhea finally reached him and hooked her arms around Saahil's neck.

'How about we go on our first date and take it from there?' she whispered looking straight into his eyes.

'A date?' Saahil smiled as he looked at her. 'Yes, I can do that.'

He seemed to suddenly realize the close proximity of their bodies and his eyes fixed upon Rhea's lips.

'Open up,' he whispered before his came lips came down on hers. After what felt like an eternity, he slipped his tongue in, and Rhea moaned.

Her dream had turned into reality.

Rhea felt herself smile against Saahil's lips.

eleven

Rhea sighed for the umpteenth time.

Tonight was her first official date with Saahil and nothing was going as per her plan.

One of her professor's had decided to extend their practical sessions class by an hour and it had ruined everything. She checked her watch again. It was already 7.00 p.m.

Shit.

That meant she only had a little over an hour to look her best. Rhea fastened her pace to her building.

Saahil's message earlier in the day had been extremely cryptic:

```
Be ready by 8.30. Dress fancy.
```

What did he mean by 'dress fancy'? How fancy were we talking about here? Meet the Queen fancy or go a nice restaurant fancy?

It was infuriating how dumb boys could be sometimes.

Rhea quickly rushed into her room and rummaged through her closet.

Where is it? Where the hell is it?

After an eternity, Rhea finally found the black floor-length dress that she'd designed herself. It was off-shoulder and cinched at the waist, which made her look thinner than she actually was.

This would have to do.

After what probably was the fastest record for getting dressed in history, Rhea breathed a sigh of relief. There were still minutes to spare.

Rhea decided to call her mother on Skype and waited for her to answer.

'Rhea? Hi, beta,' Simran answered.

'Hi, Mom. Please enable your video camera. I need your opinion on something,' Rhea said in exasperation.

'Okay. Hold on,' Simran said. 'Oh, wow. You look phenomenal.'

'Really? You think it looks good?' Rhea turned around to give her mother the full view.

'Yes, you look amazing! Where are you off to?' Simran enquired.

'I have a date!' Rhea announced.

'Really? With a boy?' Simran asked.

Rhea grinned, 'Yes, with a boy. I've given up on women for the moment.'

'You're funny,' Simran commented. 'Who's the lucky guy?'

'Saahil,' Rhea informed.

'Saahil? Isn't he the one you hated?' Simran asked, shocked.

'Yes. But…he's grown on me,' Rhea blushed.

'Wow. You're blushing. Well, hope you have a good time, beta. I have a suggestion, though. Tie your hair. It'll look great with the dress,' Simran said.

Hmm. Her mother did have a point.

Rhea quickly tied her hair into a high ponytail, just as her phone rang.

Saahil had arrived.

'Okay, Mom, I'm off. I love you,' Rhea said before disconnecting the Skype call.

Now, if only, she could get the butterflies in her stomach to calm down.

'Wow,' Saahil said as Rhea walked up to him.

His eyes checked her out from head to toe, and when he finally met her gaze, there was a deep hunger within them.

'You look amazing,' Saahil said.

'Thanks. You don't look so bad yourself,' Rhea said smilingly.

Saahil was dressed in a blazer and pants, and looked extremely hot. This was the first time she'd seen him in a formal attire, and it suited him perfectly.

Rhea started to open the passenger door of his sports car, but he took her hand away.

'What's the hurry?' Saahil asked.

He slipped his arms around her waist and touched his lips to hers. With her sky-high heels, they were almost the same height.

Rhea gently let her hand glide into his hair and pulled him closer to deepen the kiss. It felt like days had passed when they finally came up for air.

'Now, *that*, was even more amazing,' Saahil commented. His arms were still around her.

Rhea laughed, 'Let's go. We're getting late.'

Saahil nodded. He finally let her get into the car and they sped off.

'So, where are we going?' Rhea asked.

She was still shaken by the kiss and tried to focus on the present. Saahil was a better kisser than she'd imagined.

'Well, eventually, we're going for dinner,' Saahil replied.

'What do you mean "eventually"?' Rhea asked, confused.

'It means that we have to make a tiny pit stop first and

then we'll go for dinner,' Saahil explained.

He swerved the car to the left and they went down a lane with tall trees on each side.

'Pit stop? What pit stop?' Rhea repeated.

Saahil sighed, 'Rhea. You don't need to know everything, you know. I know that smart brain of yours can't help knowing everything, but just relax, and enjoy the ride. We're almost there.'

Now it was Rhea's turn to sigh. He was right. She couldn't just sit back and relax, not knowing where they were going.

After an eternity of trying to guess where they might be making the pit stop, the car pulled up to a property with tall black gates at the entrance. Saahil opened his car window, and spoke into the intercom attached to the gate, 'Hi. It's Saahil Kapoor.'

The gates opened magically and Rhea observed that they'd entered a palatial property. The house itself was massive, and there was an endless garden surrounding it. The fountain in the middle added a sense of grandeur to the property.

'Where in the world are we?' Rhea wondered.

'Just hold on,' Saahil replied.

He parked the car at the entrance of the house, and opened her passenger door. Saahil had a small smile on his face, like he knew something and wasn't telling her.

Enough with the suspense, already!

Rhea decided to keep quiet and followed Saahil to the main door of the house. He rang the doorbell and waited for someone to answer.

She looked up at his face, but his expression didn't give anything away.

Suddenly, the doors opened, and Rhea felt her mouth fall

open with shock. Her brain had officially stopped functioning because she couldn't register what she was seeing.

Standing in front of her, smiling, was none other than Christianne mon Fallinger!

Oh. My. God.

Rhea stood transfixed in front of the open door. She couldn't believe that Christianne mon Fallinger was actually standing in front of her.

Saahil laughed next to her, 'We'll have to excuse Rhea till she gets over the shock, Christianne. She's having her fan moment.'

Christianne laughed as well and enveloped Rhea in a big hug. 'Welcome, my dear. It's wonderful to meet you both!'

Finally, Rhea's brain started functioning and she hugged her in return. It wasn't every day that one got the chance to hug a legendary fashion designer.

As Christianne walked into the house, Rhea turned to Saahil, 'I can't believe this! I can't believe that you remembered the tiny piece of information that I'd told you the first time we met! How did you manage to pull this off?'

Rhea could have kissed Saahil right there, but she knew it would be a tad inappropriate.

'Do you remember my friend, Colin? She's his godmother. So, in terms of pulling it off, it wasn't difficult at all. Now, keeping it from *you*, that was difficult,' Saahil smirked.

'Lemon tea for everyone,' Christianne walked back toward them as she instructed her staff.

This was predictable. Rhea had read in an interview that Christianne served lemon tea to all her guests upon arrival.

She was a tiny woman but looked much younger than her 70 years. She was dressed in a floor-length kaftan and looked every bit the glamorous woman that the world knew she was.

'Welcome, dears,' she said smilingly. 'You've got a gorgeous one right here, boy.'

'Thanks, ma'am. Don't I know it,' Saahil smiled.

'Rhea. You look absolutely beautiful, my dear. I love your dress! What label are you wearing?' Christianne asked in her heavily accented voice.

'Actually, I designed it myself, Christianne,' Rhea admitted.

'Oh, wonderful! It's absolutely wonderful. Come, I'll give you a tour,' Christianne said to Rhea.

As Saahil took a step forward as well, Christianne stopped him.

'Run along, you. The tour is only for Rhea. I'm sure you can find something else to do,' she winked at him.

'Oh. Okay. Cool. I'll just be by the bar, I guess,' Saahil replied. He looked forlorn that he'd been banished from their company.

His eyes met Rhea's briefly and she saw the same hunger in them that she'd witnessed earlier.

Her stomach took a dive but Rhea tried to calm herself. She was with Christianne mon Fallinger. This was literally a once-in-a-lifetime opportunity.

Christianne took her up the winding stairs to a huge room that had hundreds and hundreds of clothes lined up neatly on racks. 'I thought I'll give you a tour of my personal studio, dear,' she smiled.

'I would like nothing better, thank you,' Rhea smiled back.

Her mind had gone numb again. She was actually standing in Christianne mon Fallinger's personal studio.

'Rhea, I take it you're studying fashion designing? Saahil filled me in when we spoke earlier,' Christianne said.

'Yes, ma'am,' Rhea replied. 'I was interning with an Indian designer before starting my masters' programme at LCF. I want to start my own brand when I return to India.'

'India is such a huge market now. I would love to collaborate with one of the designers there, but haven't found anything interesting yet. Oh, wait, I must show you "the dress",' Christianne said.

She pressed a button and out of nowhere, a mannequin with a floor-length dress on it materialized. Rhea realized that it was the same iconic red and white floor-length dress with which the designer had emerged on the fashion scene.

'Wow,' Rhea breathed. 'I can't believe I'm actually in the same room as this dress.'

'Yes,' Christianne smiled fondly. 'I had actually forgotten about this dress for the longest time. It's been almost 55 years since I made it.'

She looked over at Rhea and continued with a smile, 'Would you like to know how I began my journey, dear? I had initially designed a sleeveless top and a long skirt. And then, one day, I decided to combine the two! And so emerged this particular floor-length dress. The Vogue editor at the time had decided to interview me, and when I presented this dress to her, she was blown away. Soon after that, I was selling at least 20,000 floor-length dresses a month. And thus, Christianne mon Fallinger the brand, was born.'

Rhea was staring at her idol in awe. To actually hear her life story in person was beyond mesmerizing.

Christianne kept talking, 'I never knew that I would become the pioneer of modern-day dresses. Doesn't mean that I didn't see the downfall. My brand took a hit when there was a sudden influx of new designers on the scene. The biggest lesson that I can pass on to you, Rhea, is to not be buckled down by failure. You will face it at some point—you're only human. If you let the failure get to you, you're done. The fight is to acknowledge the problem and rise out of it. Once I knew that I needed to modernize my designs to compete with the new competition, my brand saw success once again.'

'You are absolutely amazing, Christianne,' Rhea managed to say.

Christianne laughed, 'Take it all in, Rhea. See this huge room full of clothes. One day, this will be you. I know you have talent. That dress you're wearing speaks volume of your talent. You have what it takes to make it big, trust me.'

Rhea blushed. She couldn't believe Christianne was complimenting her work.

'Thank you. That means a lot,' Rhea said to her idol.

'Another piece of advice. Always find new things to inspire yourself. The world is your oyster—there's so much out there that we don't know about. You can find inspiration in even the smallest of things. Don't let yourself fall into a rut, dear. You just need to test your own limits and go beyond them,' Christianne said.

Rhea nodded. She had reached another level of respect for the designer in front of her.

'Now, come. That boyfriend of yours must be getting antsy. I saw the way he was devouring you with his eyes earlier!' Christianne exclaimed.

twelve

'I still can't believe that actually happened,' Rhea commented as they walked out of Cipriani.

The Italian restaurant had been out of this world, but Rhea was still on cloud nine after having met her fashion idol. Plus, the two glasses of wine she'd had with her pasta was making her giddier than usual.

Saahil laughed, 'I'm glad you enjoyed meeting her.'

They'd stayed at Christianne's house for another hour or so during which she had shown Rhea all her trend-setting designs. This had been followed by more career advice and ideas related to what Rhea could do after graduating. They had finally left after Saahil's eyes had glazed over, signalling extreme boredom.

Rhea had left her house feeling like a brand-new person. Her mind was already brimming with multiple new ideas for her final design project at LCF.

Saahil handed his car parking slip to the valet and waited for the car to pull up to the entrance of the restaurant. 'So... how was I?'

When Rhea looked at him questioningly, he elaborated, 'How was I as your boyfriend on our first date?'

Rhea threw her head back and laughed, 'Oh, you were spectacular, Mr Kapoor. You exceeded my expectations.'

Saahil smiled, 'I'm glad. So, what now? Are you tired?'

'Tired? I'm so exhilarated I could go to the moon right

now!' Rhea exclaimed happily.

'Maybe we should leave that to date number two, Rhea,' Saahil said drily.

Rhea laughed. She still couldn't comprehend that Saahil had arranged such a special thing for her.

She suddenly leaned over and kissed him. Before she could pull away, he caught a hold of her long hair and held her in place.

Rhea cleared her throat, 'I just wanted to say thanks. I can't believe you did that. It was the sweetest thing ever.'

The car pulled up to the porch and they settled themselves into their seats.

'Hey, I'm taking this boyfriend thing seriously. I wanted you to remember our first date,' Saahil smiled.

'So…um. Should we go to your place? I don't mind another glass of wine,' Rhea stated.

She didn't want to leave Saahil just yet. All the subtle ways he'd touched her all night had made her want more.

'Whatever you say,' Saahil smiled again.

They reached Saahil's apartment in less than five minutes. Just as she was stepping out of the car, the sole of one of her heels gave way.

'Oh, no!' Rhea cried out in pain as her foot lost balance. 'My shoe!'

'Shit,' Saahil said as he lifted the shoe and examined the damage. 'Please tell me you weren't very attached to this shoe.'

Rhea laughed lightly, 'No, it's okay. I guess I have to walk barefoot all the way up there.'

Saahil picked her up swiftly in the next second, 'There's absolutely no need for that.'

'Saahil! Let me down!' Rhea said in panic.

'Why?' He looked down at her with the hint of a grin.

'Because... I'm...' Rhea began.

'Yes?' Saahil prompted. He threw her heels in the backseat of his car.

'Nothing. Lead the way,' she said. Rhea rested her head on his shoulder and closed her eyes.

This felt wonderful. She wondered why people didn't carry each other around all the time.

Saahil threw his car key at the apartment doorman, 'I'll take it tomorrow, Sarge.'

Sarge was obviously very used to Saahil's ways so he just nodded and pressed the elevator button for them.

As soon as they were enclosed in the tiny elevator space, Saahil kissed her deeply. His lips and tongue kept on coming back to her till Rhea couldn't breathe.

'Press the button,' Rhea whispered.

'Huh?' Saahil said.

'The button. To your floor,' she said again.

'Right,' Saahil shifted her around and pressed his floor button.

Now, it was Rhea's turn to grab Saahil's head and pull him toward her. She caught his lower lip between her teeth and sucked on it till Saahil's eyes clouded over.

He set her down and pushed Rhea against the elevator mirror. While his mouth ran down her neck, his hand found her breast and started gently pressing them.

Rhea moaned. The way his fingers were pulling on her nipple was turning her on so much that she couldn't bear it anymore.

Out of the corner of her eye, she could see that the elevator buttons were opening and shutting. They had apparently reached their destination a while back.

'Saahil,' Rhea moaned. 'We need to go.'

'Go? Go where?' Saahil repeated.

'Your apartment,' Rhea informed him with heavy lidded eyes.

'Come on,' Saahil grabbed her hand and led her to his apartment in such a hurry that Rhea started laughing.

As soon as they shut the door, Saahil took Rhea by the waist and pulled her toward him. 'Are things moving too fast for you?' he whispered.

Rhea shook her head no. 'Things are perfect.'

Rhea took a step back and unhooked the clasp that was holding her dress in place. As soon as she unhooked it, it fell into a puddle at her feet.

Saahil drank in the sight of her with his hungry eyes. She was wearing a strapless black bra and a black lacy thong. Her black undergarments stood out against her fair skin.

'Come here,' Saahil murmured.

Rhea walked toward him and took the blazer off his wide shoulders. Next, she unbuttoned each and every button on his shirt while staring deep into his eyes.

Saahil kissed her again and freed her hair of the ponytail.

Rhea was so lost in the kiss that she didn't even notice that he'd unhooked her bra. He pulled them backward till Saahil was seated on his couch. Rhea straddled his lap and pulled his head toward her neck.

'Suck on my neck,' Rhea ordered in a throaty voice.

'Gladly,' Saahil replied.

He moved his mouth to her neck and sucked hard. Rhea threw her head back and moaned loudly.

Saahil moved his mouth to her freed breast and took her

nipple in his mouth. He licked the nipple before sucking on it. Saahil sucked on both her nipples for such a long time that she thought she was going to come just from that alone.

Rhea grabbed his hand and moved it to her panties.

While still licking her nipple, Saahil shoved his hand inside her thong and started stroking her clitoris.

Rhea moaned again.

Saahil slipped a finger inside her till she was so wet that she couldn't handle it.

'Oh, God, Saahil!' Rhea screamed.

At her scream, Saahil slipped another finger inside her and worked her till Rhea screamed again and came all over his fingers.

'That was amazing,' Rhea panted.

'We're nowhere close to being done yet,' Saahil whispered as he pushed Rhea backward on the couch.

He quickly took her panties off her and pushed her legs open.

He met her eyes before lowering his face between her thighs. Saahil licked her inner thighs till Rhea was wiggling again in anticipation.

Finally, he opened his mouth and licked her clitoris.

'That feels so good,' Rhea moaned. 'Do it again.'

Saahil slipped his tongue deep inside her till Rhea screamed once again. He kept on repeating the action of licking and sucking on her clit till Rhea arched her back off the couch and came all over his tongue.

'Wow. That...was something,' Rhea panted again.

Saahil quickly unbuttoned his pants and stepped out of them. Rhea could see that he had a massive hard on through his boxers.

He removed a condom from his pants' back pocket and slipped it on.

Just before he was about to push into her, Saahil stopped.

'What's wrong? Why did you stop?' Rhea asked, confused.

'Rhea, I'm sorry. Please forgive me. Are you sure about this?' Saahil asked.

'About sex? Yes, I'm sure, Saahil. It's not my first time. That ship sailed a long time ago,' Rhea replied. 'Now, please, I want you inside me.'

Saahil gave a short laugh and lowered himself toward Rhea. He worked himself in till he was completely inside her.

'You feel amazing. God, you're so tight,' he whispered.

Rhea's only response was a moan.

Saahil started to move slowly inside her first and then picked up momentum.

'That feels so good, Saahil. Don't stop,' Rhea managed to say.

'Never,' Saahil replied.

He kept on thrusting inside her till they both climaxed at almost the same time.

Saahil lay down on the couch next to Rhea and pulled her toward him so that they were face to face.

'Wow,' he said.

'Yes, wow,' Rhea repeated smilingly.

'Did you come?' He asked.

'Oh, yes. All three times,' Rhea stated.

'Was it good for you?' Saahil enquired.

'Saahil. It was amazing. Trust me,' Rhea said.

Saahil chuckled when he noticed her neck, 'Ms Singh, you have an extremely huge love bite on your neck. Serves you right after instructing me to turn into a vampire!'

Rhea groaned, 'Shit. I'll have to put a lot of concealer on that in order to hide it from all my professors.'

Saahil was playing with her nipple again and giving her goose bumps. She tried to push his hand away but he was having none of it.

'This was an amazing first date. Thank you,' Saahil said as he lightly kissed her.

'Well, I normally don't put out on the first date, but…you're special, Saahil Kapoor,' Rhea said before kissing him back.

thirteen

'I hate being back in Mumbai,' Saahil complained over the phone.

He was sitting in one of the cubicles in his father's office and regretting every second of it. His father was extremely strict when it came to Saahil's work regimen, and if Saahil didn't comply with the office rules, he would have double the work the following day.

'Oh, come on. It's not so bad,' Rhea replied.

'It's pretty bad. I don't get to see you often enough in Mumbai,' Saahil commented.

He was pretty sure Rhea was smiling when she replied, 'That's true. We'll be back in London in ten days, so just… be patient.'

'Yeah, I guess,' he said. 'If I don't die with this workload before that.'

Saahil's work hours were 9.00 a.m. to 8.00 p.m. By the time he got back home, he was so tired that all he did was sleep. Therefore, he had hardly seen Rhea during their time in Mumbai.

He could go to his father and ask him to ease up on his work hours, but that would entail talking to him apart from the regular pleasantries. Saahil had barely spoken to him ever since he'd gotten back home. They were both still smarting from the fight in London.

'You'll be fine. I miss you,' Rhea said.

'I miss you too. God, you're like fifteen minutes away from me and I've barely seen you. I hate this,' Saahil declared.

'Come over post work?' Rhea asked.

Saahil could see from the corner of his eye that someone was coming to his cubicle. Talking on the cell phone for personal reasons was banned in the office, and if Saahil was caught breaking the rule, he was royally fucked.

'Okay. Gotta go now. Bye,' Saahil hung up quickly.

He saw that his father was approaching the cubicle. Saahil groaned inwardly. He really wasn't in the mood to talk to him.

Manan cleared his throat. He stood around awkwardly, waiting for Saahil to say something.

Saahil sighed, 'Hi, Dad.'

Manan seemed to be slightly relieved that Saahil had spoken first.

He replied, 'Hi. Everything going okay?'

'Yes, everything is fine. Mr Sharma is taking good care of me,' Saahil stated.

Mr Sharma was Saahil's supervisor and taskmaster.

He was worse than Hitler.

'Good. That's good. I'm glad you joined office,' Manan commented.

'Yep,' Saahil confirmed.

Both of them fell silent. They had officially run out of small talk.

'So...um, Saahil, I want to ask something of you,' Manan began.

Here we go again.

Even before his father had said whatever that he was going to say, Saahil knew exactly what it was.

'I'm sorry about London. Things didn't go the way I wanted

to convey them to you. It's my fault that I sprang the news on you like that, Saahil. Please forgive me,' Manan said quietly.

Saahil hadn't expected him to apologize. This was a first.

It's not like his father had never had girlfriends before this. But, this was the first time that he'd ever tried introducing one to Saahil. It had completely thrown him off balance. Knowing his father dated was one thing, but actually facing it was a whole new ball game.

'It's okay, Dad. I overreacted as well,' Saahil admitted.

'Okay. Good. I'm bringing this up again…but will you please have dinner with Nandini and me tonight? We would both love it. Please, Saahil. Just meet her. For my sake,' Manan pleaded.

Saahil's first reaction was to say no outright, but his father looked so worried and genuinely sincere, that Saahil felt sorry for him.

He sighed again, 'Okay, Dad. One dinner. That's it.'

It was just dinner. He wasn't betraying his mother by going out for dinner, was he?

Should his mother feel betrayed?

Before Saahil could question himself, Manan's face broke out into a big smile, 'Oh, thank you, Saahil. This is great news. I'm so happy. Great. So, I'll see you at home? We'll leave at 8.30 sharp!'

There was a spring in his father's step as he walked away.

Shit. What had he landed himself into?

⁂

'Saahil, what would you like to drink?' Nandini asked him.

They were seated at a private dining room at Hakkasan. Saahil was highly regretting the fact that they'd chosen to sit in the private section. At least if there was noise around, Saahil could block out the conversation he didn't want to hear.

'I'll have a single malt, thanks,' Saahil replied.

Nandini quickly relayed his order to the waiter and smiled at him. She was dressed in a powder-blue pantsuit and looked every bit the Mumbai socialite.

His father sat at the other end of the round table. His expressions were shifting between looking worried and relaxed.

'So, Saahil. How's college going?' Nandini asked.

'Good. Aren't you going to have something to drink?' Saahil asked her.

'Oh, no. I don't drink,' Nandini replied.

Interesting.

'So…um…do you know about his…' Saahil looked at Manan, unsure of whether he should bring up his father's past.

'You mean Manan's drinking problem? Of course I know about it, Saahil. Your father mentioned it to me the first time we met. I have no problems with it. I'm a firm believer in the idea that circumstances matter a lot in our decision-making. But, as time passes, we look at things differently and change out behaviour accordingly. I don't know what your father was going through at the time, but I think he's made a lot of changes to his lifestyle since then,' Nandini said.

She looked at Manan fondly and a look passed between them.

'You're right. I never thought of it in that way,' Saahil said grudgingly.

He didn't want to agree with his father's girlfriend, but she was right.

As Saahil's drink arrived along with Manan's fresh lime soda, they quickly placed their order for the appetizers.

'Would you like me to dim the lights?' The waiter asked.
No, please!
'No, that's okay, we're fine,' Saahil said quickly.
'Okay. Thank you,' the waiter replied and walked away.
'How is work going, Saahil?' Nandini asked.
'It's going well. Dad definitely runs a tight ship,' Saahil commented with a sideways glance at his father.

He saw his father turn a shade of deep red and grinned to himself.

'Sorry. I think. But, it's for your own good,' Manan said quietly.

'You know, Saahil, when I was about your age, my father used to be equally hard on me. My family has been in publishing for a very long time, and as soon as I turned eighteen, I was ordered to go work in our office. I used to hate my father for making me work long hours—all of my friends used to chill and relax, whereas I was in the office from 8.00 a.m. to 8.00 p.m. But now that I look back upon that time, I am so grateful for the level of discipline he instilled in me. If someone tells me to leave office early now, I blow my fuse off. Tonight is an exception, of course. I was very excited to meet you,' Nandini described with a laugh.

Saahil was having a hard time containing his shock. In the past, his father had only dated women whose sole interest in life was to shop. Nandini was a pleasant surprise. She was more than just a socialite.

'You're right. I hope I'm as grateful as you are,' Saahil replied.

Manan was now staring at Nandini with admiration and affection.

As the appetizers arrived, the conversation lulled in the middle while they feasted on a selection of assorted dim sums.

'Tell me, Manan,' Nandini said. 'How many girlfriends of yours have met Saahil earlier?'

Manan turned a shade redder than even earlier. His face marginally relaxed when he saw Nandini laughing.

Saahil couldn't stop chuckling to himself. She had managed to make his father squirm in his shoes and that was something.

'Relax, Manan, I'm just messing with you,' she told him in between bites. Turning to Saahil, she continued, 'You know, Saahil, I was warned about your father before I started dating him. All the women of Mumbai warned me against him. I was told a lot of horror stories regarding his "sordid" past.'

'Why did you decide to go out with him, then?' Saahil asked her.

She thought a moment before answering, 'I don't know. I had a feeling about him and I just went with my gut. You never know what lies beneath a tough exterior.'

Manan shook his head in disgust, 'Women have too much time on their hands. How can they just pass judgements like that?'

Nandini rolled her eyes, 'Manan. Stop it. You know that at least 75 per cent of whatever they said is true.'

That stopped Manan from continuing his rant further.

Saahil didn't want to admit it, but he was starting to think that Nandini wasn't so bad after all.

'Would you like a refill, Saahil?' Nandini asked when he noticed his empty glass.

'No, I'm good. Thank you,' Saahil replied. He felt slightly out of place being the only one at the table drinking.

Nandini smiled again and leaned slightly forward while speaking, 'Saahil, I know we got off to a rocky start. But, I'm so glad we did this. You have no idea how important it is for me to know Manan's family. If things are getting serious between us, I want to make sure I get along with his family as well. This is the reason why I kept on forcing Manan to make me meet you. Thank you.'

Saahil felt the bottom drop out from his stomach. He forced himself to nod at her.

'Okay, boys, I need to use the restroom. I'll be right back,' Nandini announced and excused herself.

'It's going pretty well, isn't it?' Manan asked Saahil eagerly.

'I can't believe it. I just can't believe that I fell for it again,' Saahil said in disbelief.

He was so stupid. So fucking stupid.

'Wh-What do you mean, Saahil?' Manan sputtered.

'I'm so dumb. I'm so dumb to let myself think that for a change, *my* approval mattered to you. I thought that maybe you wanted my blessing or something for dating Nandini. But, obviously that wasn't the case. It was *she* who needed to meet me. Not the other way round!' Saahil shouted.

Manan looked shocked. His mouth was hanging to the floor.

'You're so selfish, Dad. Everything needs to work out in your favour. And when things don't, you manipulate everyone to make sure that they do. You made me meet her even when I didn't want to. Did you ever stop to consider my wish? No. Just because your precious girlfriend wanted to vet your family, you made sure I met her! You didn't want to wreck your relationship with her and made sure I wasn't the one to cause it. Well, you know what, Dad? I'm done. I'm fucking done. Have fun explaining that,' Saahil said as he threw his napkin on the table.

He didn't care that he was swearing in front of his father.

All he knew was that he needed to get out from there.

'Now, Saahil, just—'

'Bye, Dad,' Saahil said, walking off without even looking at his father.

He'd managed to walk away even before the main course. Typical.

fourteen

Saahil rang the doorbell to Rhea's apartment and waited for someone to open the door.

He rested his forehead on the door and closed his eyes. Saahil felt exhausted.

Suddenly, the door opened and Saahil stumbled forward.

'Shit!' he shouted.

'And who are you?' An amused voice said.

Saahil turned around and found himself facing an older but spitting image of Rhea. This had to be her mother.

'Who is it, Mom?' Saahil heard Rhea shout from within.

'Hi. I'm Saahil,' he replied.

Simran let out a prolonged 'oh' and continued, 'I've heard a lot about you, Saahil. Nice to meet you.'

Saahil smiled, 'Right back at you, ma'am. And I really hope you've heard good things.'

Simran laughed, 'Very good things. Come on in. If we'd known you were coming, we would have ordered more pizza!'

They walked over to the living room where Rhea was sitting on the couch, eating a slice of pizza.

She was dressed in shorts and a t-shirt, with her hair tied in a messy ponytail. She looked so cute that all Saahil wanted to do was hold her.

'Hi!' she said, surprised. 'I didn't know you were coming!'

'Well, you told me to come over tonight, remember?' Saahil replied smilingly.

'But, we didn't speak after that...' Rhea began.

'Oh God, Rhea, let the poor boy relax. Sit, Saahil. Make yourself comfortable. I'll be right back, guys,' Simran said as she went outside.

Finally, he had Rhea all to himself.

Saahil rushed over to where Rhea sat and gave her a light kiss. 'Hi.'

'Saahil! My mother is right there!' Rhea hissed.

'Sorry. I just needed that,' Saahil admitted.

He sighed and settled down next to Rhea on the couch. Looking around the room, Saahil observed that it was extremely cozy, with the sink in sofa and a rug placed on the floor. The television unit was directly in front of the sofa, making it an ideal spot to spend lazy nights.

According to Saahil, it was better than his touch-me-not articulately designed house.

'What happened, Saahil? Is everything okay?' Rhea asked in a concerned voice.

'Yes, everything's fine. I just needed to see you, that's all. It's been a long day,' Saahil replied.

He was dying to hold Rhea's hand but it would be a tad inappropriate with her mother in the near vicinity.

'Are you sure you don't want to talk about it? We can step out for a bit, if you want,' Rhea offered.

'As much as I want to spend some time alone with you, I'm pretty comfortable here on this couch. It's perfect,' Saahil smiled.

Saahil heard footsteps approaching and shifted slightly further away from Rhea. He didn't want her mother to hate him on their first meeting.

Simran re-entered and sat down on a chair that was kept

nearby. 'Rhea, what should we feed Saahil?' She asked her daughter.

'We can order more pizza,' Rhea suggested.

'Or Chinese. Or maybe Thai,' Simran said.

'Nah. Some pasta?' Rhea asked.

'Maybe he wants Indian food,' Simran commented.

Saahil looked back and forth between the two of them. Had they forgotten that he was sitting right there?

Rhea laughed, 'This boy is incapable of eating Indian food, Mom. You won't believe what he did. I forced him to go to this Indian restaurant in London because I was missing Indian khaana so much. After we probably ordered the entire menu, I got down right to business of eating it all as soon as it arrived.'

'Yeah, obviously,' Simran nodded.

'However, after a while I noticed that Saahil hadn't even had a single bite. He was just shifting his food around. So, I asked him if everything was okay and if something was wrong with the food. His response was that he didn't know how to eat Indian food! Because there were so many options, he didn't know which sabji to eat with what! He went on to explain the complexities of the combinations and how he's never quite understood it,' Rhea finished.

Saahil squirmed in his seat. He didn't know where to look.

Simran was silent for a moment and then started to laugh. Pretty soon, all three of them were laughing their heads off.

'Saahil, how can you not know how to eat Indian food?' Simran asked between a fresh fit of laughter.

'I don't know, ma'am. I've always managed to survive without it, so I never...oh come on, I have no explanation for this,' Saahil chuckled.

He felt infinitely lighter. This was exactly what he needed.

'Please don't call me ma'am, Saahil! I like to think I'm slightly cooler than that,' Simran told him.

'You can call her Sim, like I do,' Rhea said breezily.

Saahil looked at her in horror and she laughed, 'I'm kidding. You can call her aunty, I guess.'

Thank God. He was in no way calling his girlfriend's mother by her name.

'Anyway. Let's get back to the original question. Saahil, what would you like to eat?' Simran asked him.

Saahil finally replied in a sheepish tone, 'Guys, to be very honest. I feel like having some macaroni and cheese.'

It was definitely a night for comfort food, and he was starving.

Rhea's face brightened, 'We have some Kraft macaroni and cheese left. Will that do?'

'It most definitely will,' Saahil smiled at her.

'Okay. One mac and cheese coming up!' Rhea announced as she got up to head to the kitchen. 'Mom, try to go easy on him.'

'I'll try. I'll definitely try,' Simran replied.

It was a delight to witness Rhea's exchanges with her mother. They were so comfortable around each other...and so drama-free.

Saahil couldn't help feeling a bit sorry for himself and it must have definitely showed on his face because Simran asked him, 'Saahil, I take it you live with your father?'

'Yes, Aunty, I do,' Saahil replied.

His face expression changed once again. This time it was one of anger and hurt.

He was thankful that Simran didn't comment upon it.

'Saahil, it's definitely not my place to say anything...but,

I just want you to know that time makes everything better. Trust me. The things that are bothering you now will probably seem frivolous after a while. Time heals all wounds,' Simran explained with a smile.

Saahil nodded, 'You're right. It's just…it gets a little hard at times.'

'I'm sure it does. But what doesn't kill you only makes you stronger, right?' Simran smiled.

Saahil chuckled, 'Absolutely. It's amazing to watch yours and Rhea's relationship. You guys are so good with each other.'

Simran smiled fondly, 'Yes, we are. I've tried to be Rhea's friend as well as her mother. I never want her to feel that she can't talk to me about stuff. I've realized that if your child feels comfortable talking to you, then you have nothing to fear. Some parents live in constant fear of what their child might be doing behind their back.'

Saahil nodded again. He couldn't relate to what she was saying. Not even a tiny bit.

His parents had never taken an active interest in his life.

He cleared his throat, 'Aunty, I wanted to say…sorry…for Rhea's father. I can't imagine what you guys have been through.'

A sad look came over Simran's face. She composed herself quickly before speaking, 'Thanks, Saahil. Not a day goes by that I don't miss him, you know? Sure, it's gotten easier now as time has passed, but I still can't believe that he's gone. I never talk about this stuff around Rhea because I don't want her to be upset. That girl is extremely strong, but when it comes to her father, she melts like butter.'

Saahil smiled—the image of Rhea melting like butter was adorable.

'I went through a rough time after he died. My husband

had been ill for a long time, Saahil. He had an autoimmune disorder that had left him extremely susceptible to all diseases. Eventually, they wore him down. That man took it like a champion, though. There wasn't a single day when he complained about his illness or feeling hopeless. He was incredibly strong,' Simran smiled sadly. 'I underwent a lot of depression post his death. I had to consult therapists to get back on track. I never disclosed the full extent of my depression and anxiety attacks to Rhea because I didn't want her to deal with it. But, eventually, I overcame it, Saahil. That's what I was trying to tell you earlier. What doesn't kill you does make you stronger. I'm a much stronger person post my husband's death. At the time, I couldn't imagine getting through it, but I did. With time, it hurts less.'

Saahil was staring at Simran in admiration. She was such an inspiration.

'Which is why I'm advising you again. Don't lose hope. Don't give up. Things will be better, Saahil. Trust me on that,' Simran stated.

Just at that moment, there was a crash from the kitchen.

Simran started to get up but Saahil motioned for her to sit back down. 'Please, relax. I'll go see what's wrong.'

It took Saahil a second to figure out where the kitchen was. Rhea was arranging the macaroni and cheese on a tray when Saahil hugged her from behind.

'Oh! You scared me,' she whispered.

'Sorry,' Saahil kissed her neck. 'Your mother is amazing.'

'Yes. Yes, she is,' Rhea smiled.

'I'm a little jealous, Ms Rhea Singh,' Saahil said as he kissed her cheek.

He was dead meat if her mother decided to enter the

kitchen right now. Saahil removed his arms from Rhea's waist and took the tray from her. The food looked amazing.

'There's nothing to be jealous about. You have an amazing mother as well. Call her and talk to her,' Rhea instructed.

'Okay. I'll call her when I leave,' Saahil promised.

'Guys! What's taking so long? You do know I'm sitting right here, right? Don't think I don't know what's going on back there!' Simran shouted from the living room.

Saahil couldn't help letting out a laugh. His earlier troubles had been long forgotten.

fifteen

'Rhea, please concentrate! I can't deal with so many customers on my own!' John shouted.

Asshole.

Ever since Rhea had turned down his invitation to have pizza, he'd been an absolute jerk. Cold stares and monosyllabic replies had become his forte.

'Yes, John. Relax,' Rhea sighed.

She'd returned to London two days ago and was still getting into the groove of things. It really didn't help that it was snowing in London while it had been just moderately pleasant in Mumbai. The contrast in the temperatures was huge.

She quickly whipped up a caramel macchiato and shouted, 'Nancy! Order's up!'

Rhea had about a half an hour left before her shift ended when John suddenly snapped at her, 'There's someone out there looking for you. Don't expect me to cover for you, Rhea. You better be back in a second.'

It took all her willpower to stop herself from punching John across the face.

Rhea wiped her hands on a napkin and walked up front. She wondered who'd come to meet her.

'Rhea! I need help.' Neha appeared out of nowhere and hugged Rhea.

Rhea felt the wind knock out of her. Neha had hugged her so ferociously.

'Whoa! Neha, what's wrong?' Rhea asked.

Neha mumbled something into Rhea's shoulder but she couldn't understand a word of what she'd said.

'What, Neha? Speak clearly, please! You're freaking me out!' Rhea exclaimed.

Neha wiped her nose on the back of her hand and sniffled. 'Can you get out of here? Let's go to a bar or something, please.'

Rhea sighed, 'Oh, crap, Neha. John won't let me leave. He's fucking mental, dude. Just because I turned him down to have pizza that night, he's made it his life's agenda to be horrible to me!'

'Men! I hate men!' Neha screamed.

'Ssshhhh! You can't scream stuff like that! Give me thirty minutes, please? I promise we'll go to a bar and talk. Just sit at one of the tables. Do you want some coffee?' Rhea asked.

'Coffee spiked with some whiskey,' Neha quipped.

'Okay, I can see that you're in a mood. I'll be done soon,' Rhea said as she left Neha to go back to work.

Half an hour went by pretty quick and Rhea collected her bag before meeting Neha out front. Neha had already called for a taxi, and they bundled inside.

'There's no way we could have walked, Rhea. It's freezing!' Neha commented. She pulled her woollen blazer closer to her chest.

'I completely agree with you. Walking in this weather would be insane.' Rhea observed that while Neha had stopped crying, she still looked really sad and upset.

'Neha, what's wrong?' Rhea asked. 'I've never seen you like this before.'

At that statement, Neha burst into tears once more.

'We've arrived, miss,' the taxi driver announced.

Neha had instructed him to take them to any local bar, and the bar that the taxi driver had chosen seemed decent enough.

'Come on. Let's go, Neha,' Rhea instructed her friend.

They paid the taxi driver and walked into the bar.

Neha managed to snag a corner booth, and Rhea heaved a sigh of relief. The bar was centrally heated.

'I'm going to get myself a glass of wine, Rhea. What do you want?' Neha asked with puffed up eyes.

'Nothing. I want nothing at all. I have a shit ton of reading to do tonight,' Rhea informed.

'Buzz kill,' Neha grumbled and went to get her wine.

'Well?' Rhea said when Neha got back to the booth. 'Are you ever going to tell me what's bothering you or do I have to guess for myself?'

'It's Karan, Rhea!' Neha shouted. 'Karan is the problem.'

'Karan? I thought stuff was going well between you guys,' Rhea said.

She was confused. Neha had never mentioned any issues them.

'Yeah, well, I thought things were great, but, apparently not,' Neha shouted again.

Rhea could see that her friend was on the verge of being hysterical again, so she quickly grabbed the wine glass and held it out to Neha. Neha took a huge sip and set the glass down.

'What seems to be the problem?' Rhea asked.

'I don't know, to be honest. He's been picking fights with me over the smallest of reasons. Trivial stuff. I don't even know what I'm doing wrong!' Neha explained.

'Oh,' Rhea said. 'Have you tried asking him what the problem is? Maybe if you ask him about it, it'll be clearer to you.'

'Rhea,' Neha sighed. 'I've tried to talk to him. But it always leads to a bigger fight. I don't remember the last time I spoke to him without getting into a fight. Plus, he's been partying so much. Not that I have a problem with that, of course. I'm a promoter of having a good time. You know that about me. But he always has a hangover when we talk...which doesn't help his disposition during a fight.'

'But...what is the main reason for fighting so much?' Rhea asked.

She so wasn't being a sensitive friend right now.

'As far as I can understand the problem—I think the distance is getting to him. He always ends up bringing up how far I am, and I never make the effort to come see him in Italy, and I don't have enough time for him,' Neha ranted.

'And what do you say to that?' Rhea asked.

Rhea really wished she didn't have so much work to do tonight. She wanted to have a glass of wine as well—this love quarrel was getting more interesting by the second.

'I'm a non-confrontational type of person, Rhea. I run away from confrontation. I mostly get silent when he says stuff like this. I mean, it is true, isn't it?' Neha asked.

'Interesting,' Rhea commented.

'What's interesting?' Neha cried in anguish.

'It's interesting that you're just putting the blame on yourself, Neha. Isn't he doing the same thing as you are? Why isn't he coming to London more often?' Rhea asked bluntly.

'You're right,' Neha replied slowly. Rhea could see the realization dawn on her face.

'Do you want to get to the bottom of this or continue having fights that make no sense whatsoever?' Rhea prompted again.

Neha was silent for a minute. She finally answered, 'Yes.

I want to clear it out. I can't handle it anymore.'

'There you go. You shouldn't be taking such crap,' Rhea stated. 'Call Karan and speak clearly about everything, Neha.'

'What? Call him right now?' Neha asked in panic.

'Neha, you have to do it eventually. He's making you miserable, isn't he?' Rhea asked.

Neha sighed, 'You're right. I haven't been able to sleep at night. I'll be right back.'

As Neha went out of the bar to talk to Karan, Rhea typed out a message on her phone to Saahil:

```
Hi. Miss you. Got done with Cafe Moreno.
Going back home. Wish I didn't have to study
tonight.
```

A couple of minutes passed and Neha still hadn't come back inside.

Didn't she realize how cold it was outside?

Rhea finally went outside to check on her and found Neha sobbing on the pavement.

'Neha! What happened?' Rhea asked in a panicked voice.

'We broke up, Rhea. I asked him the main reason behind his behaviour and he said he can't deal with long distance,' Neha sobbed.

Fuck. What a jerk!

'He said that he couldn't be with me anymore. Long distance was becoming too hard for him,' Neha continued. 'He even went to the extent of saying that we can remain "casual" and not "exclusive" anymore. Like, what the fuck? As if I want that. I'm not the casual relationship type of person, Rhea.'

Rhea nodded in understanding, 'You know I'm completely with you on that one. Maybe it's for the best that you guys ended things. You can't help it if he wants different things now. You should be proud of the fact that you stood up for yourself and got to the bottom of the problem. Otherwise, this uncertainty could've prolonged much longer.'

'I guess,' Neha sniffled. 'He was being so mean to me. Extremely mean. I wish I could have reached through the phone and punched him!'

Rhea sighed, 'Fuck him, Neha. Not literally, of course,'

That got a laugh out of her, before converting into sobs again.

Rhea continued, 'The fact that he broke up by making you think that you're to blame for not putting more of an effort into this relationship is absolute bullshit. He wanted out and he tried to pin this entire thing on you. And how could he suggest casual dating after two years of being in a committed relationship? That speaks volumes about his character. You're better off without him.'

'You're right. I'm going to find someone much better!' Neha declared.

'Yes, you will,' Rhea said.

However, that strong declaration was once again followed by a fresh fit of tears.

'Rhea, can you call us a taxi, please?' Neha said. 'I just want to be by myself right now.'

'Neha, are you sure?' Rhea asked, concerned.

'Yes, I'm sure,' Neha replied.

Rhea hailed a taxi and soon they were on their way. She dropped Neha off at her apartment first and told the driver to continue on to her building.

Rhea sighed. This had been a long night. She couldn't help but feel bad for her friend.

As the taxi pulled up to her building, she noticed that someone was sitting on the stairs.

On closer look, she saw that it was Saahil.

Rhea felt a warm tug at her heart and a smile broke out on her face as she walked toward him. 'What are you doing here, Saahil?'

'Hi, sweetheart,' Saahil murmured and kissed her lightly. 'I got your message and thought I'll surprise you.'

'You're the perfect cure for a long night,' Rhea sighed and hugged him. 'Now, how about we do some light reading?'

sixteen

'This weather sucks, guys,' Parth announced.

'Really? I think it's quite pretty,' Rhea replied.

'How in the world is freezing up to your eyeballs in snow pretty?' Parth exclaimed.

Rhea was seated at the Italian restaurant, Cecconi's Mayfair, with Saahil and his friends. She'd tried to get Neha to come as well, but she had flat out refused. It had been three weeks since her break-up with Karan, but Neha was still in the grieving process.

Rhea focussed her attention back on the dinner conversation. The wine was flowing even though they had finished dinner a while ago. However, no one was ready to leave just yet.

Rhea willed herself to enjoy the moment. She did have cause for celebration—her practical sessions' professor had given his approval on the jacket she'd designed in class today.

'Would you like a refill, Rhea?' Saahil asked. He was seated right next to her and made sure that she was perfectly aware of the fact.

'Sure, why not?' Rhea replied.

With his eyes on the rest of the table, Saahil slid his hand under the table onto Rhea's thigh. She was wearing a short dress; so all his hand met was bare skin. He continued to slide his hand upward till Rhea had caught hold of it and pushed it away. A couple more inches and he'd have caused trouble.

'Behave,' she whispered to Saahil. 'I'm only human, you know?'

Saahil chuckled and removed his hand. 'You're irresistible,' he whispered back.

'Guys. Get a room. Please,' Zahan said.

'Yeah,' Colin agreed. 'The two of you seem to be on your own private dinner.'

'Sorry, guys. No more private talk,' Rhea smiled.

Saahil picked up the bottle of red wine and poured some into Rhea's glass. He examined the label on the bottle and smiled, 'Guys, do you remember this bottle? We had it in Spain. By that bar near the beach?'

'Yeah, you're right! Fuck, now that was an insane trip!' Parth said.

'Dude, but the only reason that trip was so insane is Saahil. Our man sure made it into a trip to remember!' Colin pitched in.

'Why? How did he make it so insane?' Rhea asked.

Her curiosity had piqued and she leaned forward.

'Spain was insane, but you guys are forgetting about Greece! Saahil made that trip even better,' Zahan smirked.

They obviously hadn't heard her question.

'No, dude, Spain was crazier, for sure,' Parth disagreed.

Saahil cleared his throat, 'Maybe we should talk about something else. We don't want to bore Rhea with our stories.'

'Are you kidding? I'm dying to hear these stories!' Rhea exclaimed.

'Oh, Rhea, you're in for a treat. Your boyfriend is a crazy guy. The clubs used to shut at 10.00 a.m. because Saahil wouldn't be done partying till then! This guy can finish a bottle of hard liquor all by himself in a single night. I bow down to you, my man,' Colin said. He got up and actually bowed down to Saahil.

Parth and Zahan bellowed with laughter, while Saahil looked slightly embarrassed.

'Don't listen to them, Rhea. It wasn't an entire bottle,' Saahil said, turning his face to Rhea.

Rhea laughed, 'It's okay, Saahil. It doesn't bother me. Continue, guys. I want to know more stories.'

'So, we were at this club in Miami and there was this really famous DJ there. Well, Saahil literally got into a champagne war with him. If that DJ popped a champagne bottle, Saahil would pop two, and this continued back and forth for a while. Finally, the DJ got really angry and we were asked to leave the club!' Zahan replayed.

'Who were you with at the time, Saahil? I'm trying to remember. Was it Caroline?' Parth questioned Saahil.

Before Saahil could reply, Colin interjected, 'Nope, it wasn't Caroline, Parth. It was Simone!'

Rhea turned sideways to glance at Saahil but he had turned his face away. She loved the fact that he was so embarrassed.

The table 'ooooh'd' when Simone's name was mentioned.

'Now, that girl was crazy,' Zahan shook his head.

'Yeah, she was nuts,' Colin agreed.

'Guys,' Saahil shook his head.

'Wait, let them speak. Why was she crazy?' Rhea asked.

'First off, she was madly in love with Saahil, whereas he wasn't serious about her. They were sort of together for a while, before Saahil decided that it was time to end things. Simone did not take this well. When Saahil mentioned that they should break-up, Simone announced that she was pregnant with his child!' Zahan exclaimed.

What the fuck?

Rhea shifted uncomfortably and glanced at Saahil again. His face was bent toward the table, not saying anything.

'What happened then?' Rhea asked.

'Oh, nothing happened, of course. She was straight up lying. Her roommate came up to Saahil and confessed that Simone had made the entire thing up. Once she was confronted, Simone admitted to lying and we bid her adieu,' Colin finished.

Rhea let out a sigh of relief. She couldn't have handled it if Saahil had a child running around somewhere.

'Dude, what about that psycho, Sonali?' Parth announced suddenly.

'Guys, shut up. Take someone else's case, please,' Saahil interrupted.

'Come on, dude. It's such a good story,' Parth said. He turned to Rhea and continued, 'So, Saahil was with this other girl named Sonali for a while. She's from Nottingham, as far as I remember. Anyway, she was crazy about Saahil as well. I think she'd started planning their wedding in her head—she was that serious. But, you know how Saahil is. His mindset was nowhere close to hers. So, one day, Sonali found out that there's this other girl who likes Saahil as well. She got so insecure that she forced Saahil to take a trip with her to Paris! On that entire trip, she took over a hundred pictures of the two of them and uploaded them on Facebook for the world to see. It was basically a ploy to show all the other girls that Saahil was taken!'

Rhea felt her stomach twist. This topic was definitely putting her on edge.

'When Saahil found out about this, he broke up with her

on the spot. It was goodbye for Sonali,' Zahan commented.

'Rhea. Are you okay?' Saahil asked her quietly. 'I'm so sorry about all this.'

Rhea forced herself to smile, 'I'm okay, Saahil. Don't worry about it. I know it's all in good humour.'

Zahan waved a waiter over, 'Good sir, can we have another bottle of wine?'

The waiter checked his watch and said, 'Sir, we are about to close soon...'

'Oh, come on. We're having such a good time!' Zahan said.

'I guess we can make an exception since your group is one of our regulars,' the waiter admitted. 'It'll be right out.'

'Thanks,' Zahan said as the waiter walked away. 'Now, where were we?'

'Apart from all the random one-night stands, I'm trying to remember who made it to the somewhat serious category. Oh, yes. Tina!' Colin said.

Rhea felt her heart drop. She really didn't want to hear anything more.

Saahil must have noticed Rhea's expression, because he suddenly said, 'Guys, enough. Like, what the fuck are all of you on? I'm with Rhea now, and that's all that matters. She is extremely important to me and you've managed to make her uneasy. Apologize. Right now.'

'Jeez. Sorry, Rhea. We were just having fun,' Parth apologized.

The other two nodded along with Parth and Rhea plastered a smile on her face, 'Guys, relax. I'm fine. However, I'm getting late and should be getting home. I have an early lecture tomorrow.'

As Rhea got up from her chair, Saahil pushed his chair

back. 'I'll drop you home,' he offered.

'Maybe we should cancel that extra bottle of wine. I have to get to class tomorrow as well,' Parth said sadly.

'I'll go cancel it,' Zahan offered and walked over to the bar area.

'Man, I wish I could just pull off a Saahil and blow off going to college tomorrow!' Parth exclaimed.

Wait, what?

'What are you talking about, Parth?' Rhea asked.

'Oh, you didn't know? Saahil failed two of his management classes last term. He can't tell his father that he failed because his father would literally kill him. So, Saahil lied and told his father that he was taking a couple of extra courses and will graduate four months after the actual graduation date. He will, in fact, be covering up for the courses he failed in,' Parth explained. 'Genius, I tell you! Pure genius! What an ingenious plan!'

'Rhea, shall we go?' Saahil seemed unconcerned. He obviously didn't care about failing his classes.

Rhea felt her throat close. She was so angry. She couldn't believe he'd done that.

She took a deep breath and finally said, 'Saahil, I'll see you later. I'll walk to my building.'

'Rhea, your place is really far from here. Let me drop you, please,' Saahil said in a worried tone.

'No, please,' Rhea put some distance between them. 'I'll be fine. How much do I owe for dinner?'

'I think...it's around eighty pounds per person,' Colin informed.

Fuck. How the fuck had she let herself go to such an expensive place for dinner?

Rhea quickly removed cash from her purse and kept it down on the table. There went her tips from the week at the coffee shop.

'Rhea, what's wrong?' Saahil asked urgently.

'Nothing. I'll see you later,' Rhea said and walked out of the restaurant.

seventeen

Saahil stood outside Rhea's class and waited for her to come out.

He'd been waiting on LCF's campus for over an hour now. Rhea hadn't picked up his calls or replied to his texts since last night's disastrous dinner.

Fuck!

He could kill his friends. The way they'd gone on and on about his past had been nothing less than catastrophic.

Saahil paced up and down the corridor. Time was going by extremely slow today.

Finally, he heard some movement from inside the classroom and exhaled slowly.

He really needed to talk to his girlfriend.

Saahil was still getting used to the fact that he was in an exclusive relationship. Not that he minded, of course. It was easy with Rhea.

As people started pouring out of the class, Saahil craned his neck to see where Rhea was. She was talking animatedly to her professor and smiling.

He couldn't help smiling himself when he saw her. She was such a nerd.

Sorry, correction.

She was an extremely *hot* nerd.

After what seemed like ages, she started walking toward the entrance of the room and stopped dead in her tracks when she saw him.

'Saahil,' Rhea said. 'What are you doing here?'

Saahil didn't move from his position near the entrance. All he wanted to do was kiss her and ask her to forgive him for all those things that his friends had said, but he kept a distance between them. He had no idea how she would react.

'You haven't been answering my calls. Or replying to my messages,' Saahil said quietly.

'Um,' Rhea bent her head and started fiddling with her bag. 'I had a lot of work to get done with.'

'Oh, okay. Sure,' Saahil commented.

'Yes,' Rhea said.

They stood silently by the door for a minute or so before Saahil broke the silence, 'Rhea. Please, let's talk. Just…please. We need to talk.'

Rhea stared at him for a long time before replying, 'Okay. Let's go to my place. It's nearer.'

Thank God. Saahil let out a sigh of relief and started walking alongside Rhea.

The walk to her building was probably the most tensed walk he'd ever experienced in his entire life. You could cut the tension with a knife—it was that thick.

Saahil had never seen this side of Rhea and it scared the fuck out of him. He tried to stop the panic rising within him.

Had he really screwed this up?

She couldn't leave him.

Not her as well.

They finally entered her room and Rhea threw her bag on the bed. 'Okay. We're here. Let's talk,' she said.

Saahil couldn't take it anymore. He needed to let it out.

'So, that's it? You're just going to break-up with me?' He said, his voice rising with every word. 'At least put me out of my misery, Rhea. I'm a big boy. I can handle it.'

Rhea's mouth fell open in shock, 'I'm sorry, what? What the hell are you talking about?'

'Right. You're going to pretend that what I'm saying isn't true. Well, I'm not dumb, Rhea. All the signs are there. You won't even make eye contact with me. You won't talk to me. What else am I supposed to think?' Saahil shouted.

He took a deep breath. He was losing control of the situation.

'Saahil, calm down! Why the fuck would you think that I'm breaking up with you, you fool?' Rhea shouted back.

Wait, what?

'Well, aren't you?' Saahil prompted her.

Maybe there was some light at the end of the tunnel, after all.

'No, I'm not. We are in the middle of a fight, that's all. I was angry—no, wait, I *am* angry—which is why I'm giving you the silent treatment. Doesn't mean that I'm breaking up with you,' Rhea exclaimed. She still looked immensely shocked by his words.

A big smile broke out on Saahil's face and before he could control himself, he leaned forward and kissed Rhea on the lips. Hard.

Before she could react, he pulled back and sat on her desk chair. 'Okay. Cool. Now, let's discuss this.'

'Wh-What was that? You can't just do that. I'm mad at you!' Rhea sputtered.

'I know, baby. I'm sorry,' Saahil murmured.

He felt like he could breathe again. She wasn't breaking up with him.

'Do you even know what I'm angry about, Saahil?' Rhea asked quietly.

She looked incredibly sombre now.

Saahil straightened in his chair and began, 'Rhea, I'm so sorry about last night. All that stuff about my past—you weren't supposed to know all the details. I would be fucking angry myself if I was in your place. And my friends—those jerks—they wouldn't take the hint. I could kill them. But, Rhea, please don't take those stories seriously. They didn't mean anything. I wasn't serious about any of those relationships. I never once told those girls that I was their boyfriend. I never told them that I wanted to be exclusive. They just got in way over their heads, Rhea. And all that stuff about my drinking? You know I've changed. You know I've cut down on my drinking.'

Rhea just stood next to him, taking in his words.

Finally she spoke, 'Saahil, I'm not angry about any of those stories. Sure, they made me uncomfortable, but any girl in my position would be uncomfortable. And we all have pasts. I know how these things work. I'm not that shallow that I would get into a major fight with you because you had a shit ton of girlfriends. No, that's not the reason. I'm angry because you lied to your father about failing those classes!'

Now, it was Saahil's turn to be shocked. This was totally not what he'd predicted.

'This is why you were so angry? You weren't angry about all those stories?' Saahil asked.

'No, I wasn't angry about all that, Saahil. Why didn't you tell me you failed those classes?' Rhea asked in anguish.

'I don't know, Rhea. I just found out yesterday that I failed two classes and I was with the guys in college, which is why they knew. I was going to tell you. I just didn't want to trouble you, I guess,' Saahil said quietly.

Rhea sat down on her bed and sighed, 'Why would you

lie to your father, Saahil?'

'He would kill me if he knew I failed, Rhea. I don't know what would happen, to be honest. We don't have a good relationship, anyway. Wouldn't look good, now, would it? If any of his business associates or people in his social circle found out,' Saahil laughed harshly. 'I didn't expect to fail, you know. After we started hanging out...I started attending lectures and turning in my assignments. I even paid attention in all those lectures. But, I guess the damage was already long done. It was too late to pull up my grades since I hadn't turned in any assignments and essays that were due from the beginning of term. You made me want to clean up my act, Rhea. I was just too late this time. You've inspired me. You're so dedicated when it comes to your education and doing something with your life. The way you are when it comes to working at the coffee shop—it's amazing. You balance college *and* your job so perfectly. You never slack. You're always motivated. I'm sorry I disappointed you.'

Rhea finally reached out and took his hand in hers. 'You shouldn't be sorry that you disappointed *me*, Saahil. You should be sorry that you disappointed *yourself*. You have so much potential. There are so many people who would kill to be in your position, and you're just throwing it all away. You say that your father would kill you if you failed. Saahil, you should be grateful that at least you *have* a father. The fact that he cares whether you fail or not. How do you know he'll be upset only because of social consequences? Maybe he'll be upset because he actually wants you to be successful in whatever you do. Have you ever considered that? Do you even know how much your education costs? No, you don't. It's because you never had to face those troubles. Well, it costs a lot, Saahil. You have no idea how grateful I am at the chance of coming to London to study. It was a dream. You need to understand its value, Saahil. I'm not saying you shouldn't have a good time. You definitely should. But, before that, you need to get your shit together. All that other stuff…it's really not worth it otherwise.'

Rhea finally sat down on the bed, exhausted. She looked like she'd gotten everything out of her chest and was spent.

Saahil was silent for a minute before he sighed, 'I'm sorry. You're right. I know I have a lot to be grateful for. I'm a total waste of space. Rhea, I promise you, I'm going to clean up my act. I'll be a better person.'

'I'm not saying you're a bad person, Saahil. Just…learn to be more appreciative, I guess,' Rhea said. She hesitated before continuing, 'You know, when my father died, I went through a tough time. My mother was in a bad place and I had to take care of her as well. I had to be strong for her and for myself. It made me realize how good my life was before tragedy struck. I guess…I made myself strong enough to go back to that place.'

Saahil couldn't say anything. He just stared at Rhea.

'You're amazing,' he finally managed to say.

She smiled sadly, 'Thanks.'

'I'm sorry, Rhea. I'm sorry for the entire night. I'm sorry you found out the way you did,' Saahil said quietly.

Rhea gave a short laugh, 'Yes, it did catch me by surprise.'

'I'm really sorry. Do you forgive me? For all of it?' Saahil asked.

'Yes. Yes, I forgive you. I'm just glad you understood what I was trying to tell you. I was already uneasy after all those stories they mentioned last night and then the college stuff just threw me over the edge,' Rhea exclaimed. She finally gave him a small smile.

Saahil pulled on Rhea's hand so that they were closer. 'So, you were affected.'

'Of course, I was affected,' Rhea sniffed. 'I didn't like those stories one bit.'

'Really? Why not?' Saahil leaned closer to her.

He was so relieved that she wasn't leaving him.

'Because you're my boyfriend and I can't stand the thought of you being with someone else,' Rhea whispered.

Saahil finally closed the distance between them and kissed her. He kissed her over and over—in a way, he was reassuring himself that she was still with him and he hadn't fucked things up.

'Saahil,' Rhea whispered.

'Yes,' Saahil said as he kissed her neck.

'Nothing. I forgot what I was saying,' Rhea managed to say.

Saahil had just bitten her neck.

'Stop it. I'm still mad at you,' Rhea moaned.

'Are you sure?' Saahil asked as he nibbled her earlobe.

'Yes. I have to get back to college,' Rhea said as she rested her forehead on Saahil's.

They both were panting and it took a minute for them to compose themselves.

'See you later tonight?' Saahil asked.

'Yes, you will,' Rhea smiled. 'What are you going to do now?'

'Well, I'm going to hit the library, miss. There's a new warden in town, and trust me, you don't want to cross her,' Saahil grinned.

Rhea laughed, 'Well, as long as it gets the job done.'

'Rhea,' Saahil said quietly. 'Thank you. No one's cared enough to tell me what's right and wrong earlier.' When he saw that she was about to speak, he held up a hand and continued, 'I just wanted to tell you…that I'm sorry about earlier. You know, when I thought you were breaking up with me. I have… issues. I just expected the worst.'

Rhea's face softened.

'Don't worry. I got your back,' Rhea whispered as she touched her lips to his.

eighteen

'Wow. That looks amazing,' a voice said from behind Rhea.

She turned around and saw that it was one of her classmates from the Fashion Media module. The lecture had just ended and Rhea was just in the middle of packing her stuff when she'd been interrupted. Rhea was having a hard time recalling her name.

'Thanks,' Rhea smiled at her.

'Hi, I'm Anna,' she introduced herself. Anna was an extremely tiny girl. If Rhea didn't know that she was in the postgraduate programme with her, she would have mistaken her for being fifteen years old.

'Rhea,' she replied.

'What exactly have you sketched, Rhea? If you don't mind me asking,' Anna asked.

Rhea looked down at the paper on which she'd drawn a bandh gala. It hadn't been part of an assignment—Rhea had felt a sudden burst of inspiration and had put it down on paper.

'Oh, this? It's a traditional Indian attire for men. I was just doodling,' Rhea laughed.

'Well, it's pretty amazing for a doodle,' Anna said in admiration. 'Have you decided to go into men's clothing after graduation?'

Interesting. Rhea had never considered men's clothing.

'I don't know,' Rhea replied. 'I've never thought about it, actually. Keeping my options open, I guess.'

'Well, you definitely should. I've been to India a couple of times to visit and I always end up browsing all the designer stores. As far as I remember, there aren't a lot of women designers who are into men's attire, right?' Anna asked.

'You're right. Only the men seem to be dominating the scene,' Rhea agreed.

'Well, you never know. You might just be the first, Rhea. The way you've sketched the collar and lapel? That's really different.'

'Thanks, Anna,' Rhea smiled.

'Let me know if you would like to meet and just discuss stuff related to design. I would love to run a couple of ideas by you,' Anna suggested.

'I would like that as well,' Rhea agreed. 'It was really nice to meet you, Anna!'

'Likewise. See you later,' Anna smiled as she walked away.

Anna had just given Rhea a whole lot to think about.

※

Rhea's phone rang as she was heading out of LCF. She saw that it Neha calling.

Rhea picked up quickly, 'Neha! Where the fuck have you been, woman? I've tried to call you so many times, but it always went unanswered! How are you?'

Neha replied in a low voice, 'Hi, Rhea. Oh God, keep the volume a bit down. It's giving me a headache.'

'Sorry. Just sheer concern for my friend, I guess,' Rhea retorted.

Neha sighed, 'I'm sorry. I'm being a bitch.'

Rhea didn't say anything. She had been so worried about Neha over the past couple of days.

'I've just been in a rut, you know? Post Karan. I've been having a hard time accepting the fact that we've broken up. Can you believe that I left him a huge ass message on his answering machine? I said so many embarrassing things that I wanted to curl up in a ball and die. That was last week. I'm still recovering from that incident,' Neha described.

Rhea groaned, 'Neha! You know you're not supposed to try to talk to him.'

'Yes, I know that, Rhea. I had a weak moment. Okay, a couple of weak moments. No, I had a *lot* of weak moments. He probably thinks he dated an absolute lunatic over the past two years,' Neha wailed in anguish. 'I need help.'

'You do need help. I'm so glad you finally called, you idiot. I've been ranting about you to my mother. How my only friend in London has disappeared off the face of this planet!' Rhea exclaimed.

'Oh, please. You have a really hot boyfriend to keep you warm at night,' Neha sniffed.

Rhea felt herself blush. Yes, she did have a really hot boyfriend.

'Stop smiling like an idiot, Rhea. How's that going, by the way?' Neha asked.

'It's going really well. It certainly has its interesting moments, though,' Rhea said, thinking of the fight they'd had after dinner at Cecconi's a couple of weeks ago.

The fight post the initial fight had been even bigger. Saahil had tried to apologize to her by buying her a diamond bracelet from Cartier. Rhea, in turn, had almost burst an artery out of anger. She'd told him that there's no way she was going to accept the bracelet, whereas he'd tried his best to make her wear it. At one point, he'd even tried to sell the idea of having sex—with her wearing only the bracelet. While the idea had its own appeal (very much like Titanic), Rhea had sent him back to Cartier to return it. She'd also told him that he could stop by the Hummingbird bakery and get her a giant red velvet cupcake back as a form of apology. Now, the make-up sex post the giant cupcake had been memorable, for sure.

'Will you come over today?' Neha asked hopefully, interrupting Rhea's thoughts. 'I miss you.'

'Yes, I'll see you in a bit. I just have to make a quick stop first. I miss you too,' Rhea said with a smile.

'Saahil?' Rhea asked as she entered his apartment.

The door of the apartment was slightly ajar. That was strange. Saahil normally kept his door properly shut.

Rhea tentatively walked into the apartment and called out Saahil's name again. With her heartbeat increasing, she inched closer to his bedroom.

She heaved a sigh of relief when she saw Saahil passed out on the bed.

As she walked closer, she saw that Saahil was in a deep sleep. He looked beyond adorable.

Rhea shoved a lock of hair away from his forehead, and was about to walk away when Saahil suddenly reached out and grabbed her hand.

'Hi, sleepyhead. Sorry. I didn't mean to wake you,' Rhea whispered.

Saahil cleared his throat and coughed. 'I don't know when I fell asleep. I've not been feeling so well. How did you get in?' he enquired.

'The door wasn't shut so I just let myself in,' Rhea explained.

She sat down on the bed next to Saahil as he lay down again and closed his eyes.

'Oh, that's strange. I ordered some food earlier, maybe I didn't shut the door properly. It must be that damn cough syrup. Making me so damn drowsy,' Saahil complained.

Rhea stroked his cheek. 'Do you know how scared I got? I thought some burglar got into the apartment or something.'

Saahil laughed, 'No. No burglars here. So, how was your day?'

Rhea's face brightened, 'Oh, I made a new friend!'

'Good for you,' Saahil laughed.

'Yes. It was good. She got me thinking about this whole new direction. I was just randomly sketching some men's clothing in class today and she really complimented my work. I don't know. It got me thinking that it could be a possible direction after graduation, you know? I'm quite excited,' Rhea admitted.

Saahil tried to reply but he ended up coughing again. The coughing turned into sneezing pretty soon, and Rhea forgot all about her future plans.

'Do you want to go to a doctor?' Rhea asked, concerned. 'You don't look so good, Saahil.'

A panicked look came over Saahil's face. 'I hate doctors. There is no fucking way I'm going to a doctor!'

'Okay, relax. No doctors,' Rhea said soothingly.

She leaned forward to kiss him but he shoved her away. 'Rhea, I'm sick. I have an awful cold and cough. You can't kiss me. I don't want to pass it on to you!'

'Oh, come on,' Rhea said.

'Nope. No way,' Saahil said as she tried to kiss him again. He turned his face into the pillow so that Rhea wouldn't have access to his mouth.

Rhea laughed. This was extremely funny.

Saahil began laughing with her and that turned into a massive coughing fit again. Rhea handed him a glass of water to soothe his throat.

'I'm sorry that I'm such terrible company. I feel like crap,' Saahil said as he shut his eyes again.

'Shut up, Saahil,' Rhea said. She leaned forward and kissed his forehead tenderly.

He looked so innocent and vulnerable all bundled up in his blankets.

'Did we have plans to meet? I can't recall,' Saahil said.

'Nope. We didn't. I just dropped by to say hi. Neha called earlier saying she wants to hang out. But, I'll tell her I need to take a rain check since you're not well,' Rhea stated.

'What? No, Rhea. You're going to go out and meet Neha. That girl has been through enough and she probably wants to vent to her friend. I'm fine. I'm not that sick, anyway. Nothing that a couple of medicines won't cure,' Saahil said.

Rhea saw that his defences were down so she quickly leaned forward and kissed him on the lips.

She laughed at Saahil's expression. 'It's okay, Saahil. I can live with a couple of germs.'

'You're crazy,' Saahil said smilingly. 'Anyway. Let's get back to the original topic. You aren't going to cancel your plans. I'm going to be terrible company tonight, anyway. I want you to go out and enjoy. Don't worry about me. I'll be fine.'

'Are you sure?' Rhea asked with her brow furrowed.

'Yes, I'm very sure. I'm going to binge play some FIFA in a bit,' Saahil said.

'Yuck,' Rhea scrunched up her face.

'Yes, exactly. You know you won't miss out on anything.

After FIFA, I plan on taking some of this cough syrup and passing out,' Saahil stated. 'It's going to be the perfect evening.'

Rhea threw up her hands, 'Okay. If you say so.'

'Yes, I do say so. Before you leave, take the spare apartment key. So you don't have any trouble entering the next time you decide on a surprise visit. The key is out there on the living room table,' Saahil informed.

Rhea smiled in response.

'Okay, now that you've kissed me...why don't you come closer and give me a proper kiss?' Saahil smiled back.

Rhea laughed and did just that.

nineteen

Saahil tossed and turned in his bed.

He tried to fall asleep, but his cough kept waking him up.

He even tried to play FIFA, but his eyes had started watering due to the onset of a slight fever, and he'd decided to come back to bed.

Saahil checked the time on his phone and saw that it was barely 10.00 p.m. No wonder he couldn't fall asleep. Saahil couldn't remember the last time he'd fallen asleep this early.

He wished Rhea were here.

He knew that he was the one who'd pushed her to go meet her friend, but he'd secretly hoped that she would stay with him.

He could sense that his mind was drudging up some memory from the past, but he stopped himself from getting too far.

Saahil typed out a message to Rhea:

`Hi.`

He waited a couple of minutes for her reply, and when it didn't arrive, he threw his phone slightly far away on the bed.

Fuck. His temperature was rising.

Saahil bundled himself even tighter in his blankets and shut his eyes.

Oh, wait. His trusty cough syrup would come in handy right about now.

Saahil took two big sips of it and set it aside.

Finally, he felt his throat calm down slightly, and shut his eyes again.

※

'Hello, Aunty. How are you?' A young Saahil asked one of his mother's friends.

'Oh my God, Saahil, beta! You've grown so tall!' Aunty exclaimed.

Saahil forced himself to smile. He felt like he was going to collapse from the effort. 'Thank you, Aunty. I'm the tallest in my class! The entire second grade is jealous of me!'

'That's amazing, beta,' Aunty said as she ruffled his hair.

'Do you know where my mother is?' Saahil asked hopefully.

'Oh, yes, Saahil. Just follow the noise! It's quite a crowd that's turned up! But then, everyone turns up to your parents' legendary parties! I'm just on my way to the bathroom and will be right there, in case anyone asks!'

Why would anyone ask a seven-year-old boy about where this aunty had gone? Saahil thought.

Saahil walked down the corridor to his living room. He felt so weak and feverish. He'd tried calling out for someone to come check up on him in his room, but everyone had seemed too busy with the party.

'Mom?' Saahil shouted feebly.

There were at least fifty people gathered in the living room, and each had a glass in their hands. While some were talking animatedly to each other, the others were dancing in the middle of the room.

'Mom?' Saahil shouted a bit more loudly.

Finally, the uncle standing closest to him noticed him shouting for his mother. 'Hello, Saahil! What's wrong?'

'Can you call my mom, please?' *Saahil asked.*

'You just hold on. I'll tell her you're here, right now!' *Uncle exclaimed boisterously over the loud noise of the room.*

Saahil craned his neck to see where his parents were. His mother was talking to some other woman, while drinking some red liquid. He saw her laugh and drop some of it. Oh, crap. She was definitely going to regret the carpet stain in the morning. His father, on the other hand, was standing extremely close to some other lady and talking with his head bent toward her.

After what seemed like an eternity, Saahil saw his mother rushing toward him. 'Saahil! What are you doing here? What have I told you about these parties? You are never to come near them!'

'Mom,' *he whispered.* 'I feel really sick.'

As his mother touched his forehead, he could smell the liquid on her. It made his stomach twist.

'You have fever, baby. Come on. Let's get you into bed. Where is your maid? She's so going to get fired for this,' *Payal said.*

'I kept calling for someone but no one came. Please, can we take Dad with us as well?' *Saahil pleaded.*

Please let's take him away from that wretched woman he's talking to, Sahil wished.

He heard his mother snort before going up to his father and saying something heatedly. Finally, they both came toward him with fake smiles on their faces.

'Son!' *Manan announced.* 'Not feeling well, beta? Don't worry. You'll be fine soon.'

Saahil could smell the same revolting liquid on his father. He felt like he was going to throw up.

Saahil tucked his hand into his mother's hand and walked with them toward his room.

'Slow down, Dad!' Saahil exclaimed. His father was walking at an extremely fast pace.

Payal gave a harsh laugh, 'You know better than to say that, Saahil. Don't you know that Daddy has stuff he needs to get back to?'

Manan stopped and turned around to look at her. 'Shut up, Payal.'

'Shut up? Why the hell should I shut up? Give me one good reason to shut up, Manan,' Payal replied.

Saahil could see that she was turning red in the face. Oh, no. This couldn't be good, Saahil thought.

He shivered and got under the blankets as soon as they entered his room.

'Payal. I'm warning you. Stop talking. You have no idea what you're talking about!' Manan shouted.

Now that they were in the safety of the room, raised voices weren't a problem.

'Do you think I'm blind, Manan? You think I don't know what you're doing? Stop trying to play the innocent card. Everyone at that party knows your antics,' Payal shouted.

'Antics? What antics? I have no idea what you're talking about, woman. Your judgement is deluded. And what glass of wine is that, Payal? Fourth? Fifth?' Manan laughed. 'Everyone in that room also knows that you can't be reasoned with after a certain number of glasses.'

Saahil shivered and tucked his blanket under his chin.

Payal scoffed, 'You're one to comment on my drinking, Manan. At least I only drink during these parties. When was the last time you slept sober?'

'Whatever. I can't deal with your nonsense,' Manan replied. He turned around to open the door when Payal caught hold of his arm roughly.

'Where do you think you're going? Back to that floozy? At least have the decency to not flirt with her openly in public. These are my friends too,' Payal hissed.

Floozy? What in the world was floozy? Saahil wondered.

'Leave me, Payal. You're treading a dangerous path,' Manan replied silently.

Payal let go of his arm immediately. She laughed, 'I have no wish to hold you, you lunatic. No wish at all. Go back out there and make a fool of yourself. I don't care! Everyone at that party will laugh at you and me. Everyone knows these women only give you attention because of the money you have. Ever tried to think what you are without that? Well, you're nothing, Manan Kapoor! Nothing at all! And, of course, they'll laugh at me too. And why shouldn't they? I turn a blind eye to all your shenanigans and couldn't be dumber!'

Manan stared at her for a minute before storming out. He shut the door loudly behind him.

'Manan! Come back here, you coward!' Payal shouted before running out after him.

The door shut behind them.

Saahil tried to block out the noise and closed his eyes.

This was so typical.

They'd forgotten about him.

Once again.

Why couldn't they ever catch him when he felt like he was going to fall apart?

'Rhea left as well, you fool,' his mind told him.

Rhea' Saahil wondered.

Catch me...Please...
'Time to wake up, Saahil.'

⌘

Saahil felt someone shaking him. He mumbled something and tried to shake off whoever was troubling him.

'Saahil. Saahil, wake up,' Rhea said as she shook his shoulder. 'You're burning up with fever.'

Saahil woke up with a start. 'Rhea?'

'Yes, it's me, Saahil. You need to take medicine. And we're going to the student health centre first thing tomorrow. I can't believe I let you get off that easily earlier. I should have pushed you to go to the doctor,' Rhea said angrily.

'What are you doing here? Didn't you go to Neha's?' Saahil said with his eyes closed.

'I did go to Neha's apartment. But, after a while, I couldn't stop worrying about you. I got your message and when I tried to call you, you didn't pick up. After that, I got really worried and came over.'

She got a wet napkin from the bathroom and placed it on his forehead. 'This should get the fever down,' she said soothingly.

She then turned her angry eyes toward him, 'Why didn't you tell me you were feeling so sick, Saahil? You said you just had a cough and cold.'

Saahil mumbled, 'I wanted you to go out and enjoy.'

Rhea seemed to get even angrier at his statement. 'Where are your medicines?'

Saahil pointed toward his drawers. He felt so weak.

She rummaged through his drawers and found a paracetamol. 'Open up,' she instructed.

Saahil gulped down the medicine with water and tried to smile, 'Thanks, Rhea. You didn't have to come back.'

Even in his feverish state, Saahil looked at Rhea to hear her response. He needed to hear what she said.

'Saahil. I'm so angry with myself for leaving in the first place. You didn't look so good when I left and I should have stayed here with you. I'm so dumb,' Rhea said.

'Still. You didn't have to come back,' Saahil repeated.

'I *wanted* to come back, Saahil. Who else is going to take care of you if not me? Now stop talking and rest. Your fever will come down soon,' Rhea ordered as she went to the bathroom to wet the napkin again.

When she came back, Saahil smiled again as she put the wet napkin on his forehead. But the remnants of the dream were still fresh in his mind, and he spoke the first thing that came into his mind. 'Rhea, can I ask you something?'

'Yes, of course,' Rhea replied, her hand still trying to arrange the wet napkin on his head.

Saahil cleared his throat before speaking hesitantly, 'Will you…catch me? When I need to be caught?'

Saahil wanted to kick himself for sounding so needy but her reply to the question was too important. He held his breath and waited for her to answer.

Rhea looked into his eyes. If his question had surprised her, she definitely didn't show it. 'Always, Saahil. I'll always be there to catch you.'

'I love you, Rhea,' Saahil said quietly.

At his words, Rhea stopped fussing over his hair for a second. She finally gave him a big smile and said, 'I love you too. Now, we need to get some food in your system! You need to fuel up, mister!'

twenty

One Year Later

'Sagar, get me the sales report of our Khopoli plant,' Saahil shouted at his secretary.

'Yes, sir!' Sagar popped his head into Saahil's cabin and disappeared.

Saahil checked his e-mail again, as was his habit during office hours. He was waiting for a couple of e-mails from his tech liaison in Bangalore.

Saahil crossed his fingers below his desk. He hoped that what he was planning would come to life soon.

'Sir, here they are,' Sagar entered the cabin and kept a sheaf of papers on Saahil's desk. 'Also, your grandmother called. Told me to tell you to call her back.'

'Okay. Thanks, Sagar,' Saahil sighed.

Ever since he'd shifted back to Mumbai, his grandparents had been overly clingy. Finally, they had someone who they could control. Since they could never put some sense of reason into his father or his mother, Saahil was the only project they could count on.

Saahil checked his watch. It was 7.45 p.m. He had to rush for dinner with a potential investor from Delhi who was flying down to Mumbai for the meeting.

'Hi, Dadi,' Saahil said into the phone when his grandmother picked up.

'Saahil, beta. When are you coming home?' Dadi shouted.

Saahil took the phone away from his ear and stared at it. *Why was it that people beyond a certain age thought that no one could hear them over the phone unless they screamed at the top of their lungs?*

'Dadi, I'll be late. I have to go out for dinner with someone from work,' Saahil explained.

'Oh, no. Your grandfather and I will be all alone again. Any idea where your father is?' Dadi asked.

'No idea, Dadi. He must be in his cabin,' Saahil stated and hung up.

Or out with his girlfriend. Don't know, and don't care.

It had been a year since Saahil had been back home in Mumbai and working for his father. Even though work was challenging, Saahil was bored out of his mind. His father's business was extremely dry—every section of the business was well sorted and Saahil was still trying to find his place in it.

Finally, after months of being sucked into the steel business, Saahil had realized what he wanted to do.

He'd come up with an app-based business idea—he wanted to recreate the beginning of Facebook. It would be an online portal that would only connect college students to each other. As soon as the student graduated from college, his or her account would be deactivated.

The idea was still in the beginning stages, and Saahil was hoping that it would see some progress soon. He hadn't shared this new venture of his with anyone yet—except Rhea, that is.

Saahil got up from his seat and stretched. He walked over to his secretary's station and said, 'Sagar, can you tell them to put my bag in the car? I'm leaving.'

'Sure, sir,' Sagar got up from his chair.

'Any idea where Dad is?' Saahil enquired.

'No, sir. I know he left a while back, if that helps,' Sagar stated.

'Okay. Thanks,' Saahil said.

The only time his father and him spoke was during office hours. Saahil couldn't remember the last time they had spoken about anything other than work.

He walked out of the office and waited for his Range Rover to be brought up to the front. As soon as it arrived, Saahil was on his way to the Four Seasons Hotel.

While he was stuck in traffic, Saahil called Rhea.

'Hello?' Rhea answered, breathlessly.

'I really hope you sound so breathless due to the fact that my voice makes your heart pound faster and you can't think straight,' Saahil stated.

'Very funny. You wish. I heard my phone ring across the room, and I had to rush over to answer it,' Rhea replied.

'You can lie all you want, sweetheart. I know what gets you off,' Saahil laughed.

'Sure. Whatever floats your boat. What's up?' Rhea asked.

Saahil could tell that she was smiling.

'I'm on my way to the Four Seasons. Have to meet this potential investor coming in from Delhi. What about you?' Saahil asked. Just hearing Rhea's voice was making all the stress of the day disappear.

Finally, the cars started moving and Saahil was on his way again.

'I'm still stuck at work. There's some big-shot coming into the store tomorrow, so we have to put out our best stuff. Everyone's really stressed out. Including me,' Rhea described.

'Who's Sukhvinder Rajput trying to impress now, man?' Saahil wondered aloud.

'Beats me. Okay, I have to go now. Call me after dinner?' Rhea asked.

'Will do. I love you,' Saahil said tenderly.

'I love you too,' Rhea answered and hung up.

Between his and Rhea's work hours, they hardly got to see each other apart from the weekends. But, Saahil made sure they made up for lost time when they were finally together.

He couldn't believe that it had been over a year since he had started dating Rhea. Saahil could say that it had been the best year of his life, hands down. He thought back to the time when he'd been scared of being anyone's boyfriend and it made him laugh. Rhea had proven him wrong.

Finally, he reached Four Seasons and handed his car over to the valet. Just as he was about to enter the hotel, his phone rang.

'Hello?' Saahil answered.

'Hello, Saahil. This is Ashwin Sehgal,' the reply came.

'Yes, Mr Sehgal. I've reached the hotel,' Saahil said to the guy he was supposed to meet.

'I just wanted to let you know that my flight has been delayed and I've just landed. I'll be there in another forty-five minutes for sure, if that's no problem,' Sehgal said.

Saahil groaned inwardly before replying, 'Sure, Mr Sehgal. Not a problem. I'll be here. Take your time.'

What the hell am I supposed to do for the next forty-five minutes now?

Saahil walked inside Café Prato, one of the hotel's restaurants, and told them about his time predicament. Thankfully, they agreed to shift his reservation for the time he gave them, and asked Saahil if he would be willing to hang out at the bar.

Saahil didn't need to be told twice to do that.

Just as he was about to cross the restaurant to go to the bar, Saahil did a double take. He wasn't sure but he could swear that he'd just seen his father at the table on the far end.

Saahil weighed his options. He could just ignore his father and head over to the bar. But, if Manan found out later that Saahil had been in the same restaurant and not met him, it would lead to an awkward conversation for sure.

Fuck it. Saahil decided to head over to his father's table.

As Saahil crossed the various other filled tables, he could see that Manan wasn't alone. He was with someone. A woman.

Oh, God. He was no mood to make small talk with Nandini right now.

Manan hadn't noticed Saahil as yet. As Saahil watched, he saw his father pick up the woman's hand and kiss it.

Disgusting.

Saahil was about to turn in the other direction, but the damage was done. His father had seen him and his expression changed from being relaxed to surprised.

'Saahil!' Manan announced.

The woman didn't turn. *Why wasn't Nandini saying anything?*

'Hi, Dad,' Saahil replied.

He finally reached them and stood between the occupants of the table.

Saahil felt the bottom of his stomach drop out.

The woman wasn't Nandini.

His father had been kissing some other woman.

Saahil acted on reflex.

He balled his hand into a fist and punched his father straight across the face.

Saahil didn't know what his father's reaction was because he headed straight back outside right after the punch. He could hear the rest of the guests panicking, and a woman's cry of anguish.

It must have been his father's date.

Saahil's brain had gone numb. He didn't want to analyse the situation till he didn't have to.

Saahil reached the entrance and asked for his car to be brought around.

Suddenly, he felt someone grab his arm roughly and turn him around.

Manan looked enraged. 'Saahil, what the hell is wrong with you?'

'I have nothing to say to you. Just go back inside,' Saahil replied coldly without meeting his father's gaze. He didn't want to see his face.

'Yeah, well, not before you explain yourself, boy!' Manan shouted. He looked as if he still couldn't believe that he'd been sucker punched in the face by his son. There was an angry pink bruise developing across his cheekbone now.

Saahil felt a weird sense of satisfaction upon seeing it.

'Who is that woman?' Saahil asked with no emotion in his tone.

'She's an associate of mine!' Manan replied.

'You mean an associate you're sleeping with,' Saahil corrected.

'Watch it, Saahil. That's none of your business,' Manan said quietly.

His eyes were still simmering with anger.

Saahil was surprised his father hadn't punched him back. He wouldn't put it past him.

Saahil threw up his hands, 'Oh, I'm sorry, of course I know it's none of my business. But, it became my business when you made me go on a dinner date with you and Nandini. Remember Nandini?'

'Stop it, Saahil. Of course I remember Nandini. She's still as important to me as she was then,' Manan informed.

'Oh, really? That wasn't the image you portrayed when you kissed that woman's hand!' Saahil retorted.

Manan sighed, 'Saahil. Please don't confuse the two. I am very serious about Nandini. This is just a random fling on the side. What's the big deal in that?' Manan looked perplexed.

Is he serious?

Saahil wanted to punch him again.

'Big deal? You're committed to her, Dad. Of course it's a big deal,' Saahil said. He felt like he was explaining the rules of the world to a five-year-old.

'Pfft! You're making this a bigger deal than it is, Saahil. There's nothing wrong with what I'm doing. And the sooner you realize this stuff, the better it is. Don't weaken yourself with all this commitment bullshit. Trust me,' Manan said.

Saahil's car had arrived a while back, but he couldn't move from his spot.

'I can't believe you,' he finally said.

'What's not to believe? I repeat—it's really not a big deal! So, I have an affair on the side. At least it keeps my relationship with Nandini on the right track,' Manan said.

He looked so serious. He genuinely believed all the crap he was saying.

'Dad. This is just wrong,' Saahil said quietly.

'Fine. Let me explain how these things work, Saahil. Now that we have broached the subject, let's get it all out. I realized a long time ago that having an affair on the side gives you the upper hand in the relationship. You aren't completely at your other half's mercy. You can detach yourself whenever you want! It's as simple as that! And it works well, son, it really does,' Manan described.

Saahil couldn't believe where this conversation had led. He knew he should just get in his car and drive off, but he couldn't.

'You mean, it gave you the upper hand with Mom,' Saahil said.

Manan looked at him for a minute. He finally said, 'I've never spoken about this with anyone earlier. But, today, I will. You think I'm the only one in my marriage who had an affair? No, I didn't, Saahil. Your mother had an affair way *before* I did. She never knew that I found out, of course. I didn't want to give her the satisfaction. But, I did find out. He was one of my close friends. The man she had an affair with. I'm sure she would have given me several excuses for having the affair—I was an inattentive husband, I drank way too much, I didn't give her enough time, etc. I didn't want to hear any of it. I didn't need to. But, I remember I was crushed when I found out, Saahil. Completely crushed. I felt so betrayed. I also remember that I hated feeling that way. I made a promise to myself after that. I promised myself that I would never feel this way ever again. And, so, I started having my own affair. That one affair led to many…and you know the rest. I've followed that promise till date, beta.'

Saahil couldn't believe what he had just heard. He wanted to laugh and cry like a maniac at the same time. What he had heard was so fucked up that he didn't know how to react. So, Saahil did the only thing he knew how to do. He shut all the emotions he was feeling inside a big box in his mind so that he didn't have to deal with it.

He composed himself and finally said, 'I still stand by my earlier notion. Commitment is important.'

Manan gave a short laugh, 'You're one to talk about commitment, Saahil. What have you ever committed to in your life? You think you were committed to your education? Do you think I'm so dumb? I know that you stayed back in London because you failed your classes in one of your terms. I know all about it. You couldn't even commit to your education. Let's move on to work. You think I don't know that you hate coming to work? I know exactly how much you hate it. These things are very simple, Saahil. Try to commit to the simple things first before moving on to bigger things.'

Saahil couldn't think of any response to that. His father's words had struck home.

'Anyway, I'm heading back inside. See you at office tomorrow.' Manan walked away, leaving Saahil stuck to his spot outside the hotel.

Was his father right? As much as he hated to admit to himself, deep down his parents' opinions really mattered to him. It was the bane of his existence.

He needed to go to his old house and play *House of the Dead*. He definitely needed to kill some zombies.

Before Saahil could walk over to his Range Rover, he heard a car pull up.

He looked up and groaned loudly.

The potential investor he was meeting from Delhi had arrived.

twenty-one

'Neha? Yeah, I'm on my way. I'll be there soon,' Rhea spoke into the phone. 'Yes, Sweetish House Mafia in Bandra West. Okay, bye.'

Rhea turned her head toward the traffic on the road. Her Uber had been stuck in traffic for the past fifteen minutes, and was finally moving ahead at tortoise speed. If she had the option of changing one thing in Mumbai, it would be the traffic. Not that Delhi had been any better. Half of the day would go by in commuting from one place to the other.

Rhea had left work early today. Neha was in Mumbai visiting some of her cousins, and they had made plans to meet for coffee.

She was really excited to meet Neha. They hadn't met since being back from London.

'*Bhaiya, idhar se left turn* (Please take a left here),' Rhea instructed the Uber driver. This was even more irritating. The male ego, of course, couldn't be tarnished. While the driver knew that Rhea was right, he didn't even acknowledge the fact that she'd spoken from the back seat.

Whatever. This crap couldn't bother her right now. Work had been kicking her ass over the past week, and she needed a break.

Working for Sukhvinder Rajput had been a dream come true. Ever since that realization in London, Rhea had started to see herself as a designer for menswear. When the time had come for job applications, Rhea had taken a chance by applying to the designing team at Sukhvinder Rajput, and it had actually paid off. They'd loved the samples and designs she'd submitted, and had offered her an amazing salary package.

It was everything Rhea could have asked for.

'*Bhaiya, idhar left pe jaana hai* (Left here)!' Rhea screamed at the driver. He'd driven right past Sweetish House Mafia.

He finally stopped in front of the café, and Rhea heaved a sigh of relief. Dealing with Mumbai roads and traffic after a hectic day of work was a pain.

'*Sorry, madam, itna traffic hota hai toh dikha nahi* (Sorry, ma'am, there is so much traffic, I didn't see)...' The driver began justifying himself.

Rhea merely shook her head, and paid him. She didn't want to get into an argument over the driver's inefficiency.

As soon as she walked in, Rhea heard someone shout her name, 'Rhea! Hi!'

Neha beamed at her from her table across the room, and Rhea couldn't help smiling herself. She rushed up to Neha and hugged her.

'It's so good to see you, Neha! I'm so happy you came to Mumbai!' Rhea exclaimed.

'I know, man. Same here. I wish I'd come earlier,' Neha replied.

They sat down on the wooden chairs, and Rhea observed that Neha was positively glowing. She'd cut her hair short as well, and it did wonders for her face.

She quickly glanced around the café and noticed a couple sitting nearby, with their eyes fixed on each other.

Saahil immediately popped into her head, and Rhea inwardly smiled to herself.

'Neha, you look amazing. What's the secret behind that glow?' Rhea quizzed, shaking off thoughts of her boyfriend.

'I don't know. I've just been in a good place, I guess,' Neha shrugged. 'Anyway, should we order something? I don't know what's good here, so I waited for you to come.'

'Oh my God, Neha. You don't know what you're missing out on. This place is paradise. Trust me, you'll know what I'm talking about in a minute,' Rhea explained.

She walked up to the counter where the sales guy was standing, and quickly ordered two nutella sea salt cookies. Her mouth was watering just thinking about them.

Rhea wondered whether to order cookies for Saahil as well, but she decided against it. She had no idea what time he was getting done from work today.

'Here you go, ma'am,' the sales guy said as he handed Rhea the cookies on a plate.

'Thank you!' Rhea exclaimed as she bounded back to the table where Neha sat.

Rhea carefully observed Neha as she ate her first bite of the cookie. She laughed as Neha's expression turned to one of pure ecstasy.

'Wow,' Neha commented. 'This is fucking good.'

'I know. Sometimes, I just come in and eat a cookie and feel all my stress fade away,' Rhea described.

'Yes, this will definitely get the job done,' Neha said with a smile. 'So, what's going on? How's the job going?'

'The job is going really great,' Rhea said.

'That's it? No more details?' Neha prompted.

'Well…it's going really well, and I'm making good money. There are no complaints in that department. It's just that…I wonder what's next. There's a small part of me that's still not completely satisfied, you know?' Rhea stated.

It was true. Rhea would catch herself feeling like something was missing in the middle of work, and it would mess with her head. Most of the time Rhea ignored this feeling, but she knew deep down that she wouldn't be able to ignore it forever.

'You'll figure it out, Rhea. It's just your first job out of college. There's a lot to come ahead,' Neha said with a flick of her hand.

'Yeah, you're right,' Rhea agreed. 'You know how stressed I get over these things, Neha. Anyway, how are things in Delhi? Enjoying being back home?'

'Yes, it's going great. I'm finally…good with things,' Neha's face darkened slightly as she spoke. 'It took me a lot longer than expected to get over Karan. I was in a bad place, Rhea. You, of all people, know that. I thought that coming back to India would be a good change, but it only made things worse in some ways. Karan and I have so many common friends in Delhi, and whoever I meet, mentions his name sometime or the other. Apparently, he's dating someone else. Some girl he met in Italy. That's the news I heard from the grapevine.'

'Oh,' Rhea paused while chewing her cookie.

'No, no, it's a good thing. After I heard that he's with someone else, my eyes finally opened. I realized that it's high time I move on as well. God knows what I've been waiting for!' Neha exclaimed.

Rhea smiled, 'Good for you, Neha. I'm so happy for you.'

Neha nodded, 'I'm happy as well. Stuff is finally falling into place. Enough about me, dude. How's Saahil?'

Rhea blushed. She just couldn't stop blushing whenever someone mentioned his name. It was sick.

Neha rolled her eyes, 'Oh God, Rhea. You're like a character from a romance novel. I take it things are going well?'

Suddenly, a loud voice rang across the café, 'Oh my God, I can't believe it!'

Rhea and Neha turned around to see the couple sitting nearby locked in an embrace. The girl was clutching her hand in front of her face and admiring the ring on her finger.

She noticed Rhea and Neha staring at her and exclaimed, 'He finally proposed! I can't believe it!'

'Congratulations!' Rhea shouted out to her happily.

She continued to stare at the happy couple till Neha whispered, 'Rhea. Stop staring!'

Turning back to Neha, she let out a happy sigh. That had been such a nice moment to witness.

'So, where were we? Yes, things are going really well. Saahil's been great, Neha. It's been…perfect,' Rhea smiled.

'Wow. You're beaming from all the love, Rhea. I'm so happy for you,' Neha said as she leaned across the table to hug Rhea. 'It's such a surprise, though. I never expected Saahil to be this way. After everything I'd heard about him…it's really nice to hear that you guys are so happy.'

Rhea laughed, 'It took him a while to completely accept the fact that he was no longer the party king that he was before. But, I think he was secretly glad to be out of that entire phase.'

From the corner of her eye, she saw the newly engaged couple exit from the café.

'Yeah, I'm sure. Being a party king sounds stressful to the core. By the way, how are his parents? Do you get along with them?' Neha enquired.

Rhea shifted around uncomfortably, 'Um…I've never met them.' She took a huge bite out of the almost demolished cookie.

Neha stared at Rhea for a minute before speaking, 'You're kidding, right?'

Rhea shook her head. 'Nope, not kidding. It's just never happened. I've been to his house numerous times, but it's only later in the night once he and I get done with work. And even then, I don't end up running into anybody. His house is so big—everyone has their own wings.'

'Haven't you ever wanted to meet them?' Neha asked. She had a knowing look on her face.

Rhea was getting more uncomfortable by the second. She didn't like where this conversation was headed.

'To be very honest...yes, I have wanted to meet them. Many times. But, Saahil is so detached from his family life, Neha. You know his parents are divorced, right? He hardly talks about them, which is why I've never had the courage to talk about meeting them,' Rhea admitted.

'Okay, don't freak out. What about marriage and stuff? Have you guys ever spoken about it? The look that came over your face when that couple got engaged spoke volumes,' Neha asked after a pause, with the knowing look still on her face.

There it was—the dreaded question.

'No, we haven't spoken about it. But, there's no need to bring it up right now, Neha. Marriage is the last thing on our minds. Besides, Mom has never pressured me to get married. She's told me multiple times that it's completely up to me when I want to get married,' Rhea said.

Neha nodded, 'That's completely understandable. Tell me something, Rhea. Can you see yourself married to Saahil?'

Rhea knew the answer to that. She'd thought about it multiple times. As modern as her thinking was...she wasn't immune to the dream of getting her happily-ever-after ending.

She wanted that same ecstatic feeling the girl who'd just gotten engaged in the café had experienced—the ultimate commitment from the person you loved with your entire heart.

'Yes, I can. I do want to get married to him, eventually,' Rhea answered with a smile. There was no point in denying it.

Neha let out a huge 'aawww' and Rhea blushed again. She used to be the last person who went all gooey over a boy, but Saahil had turned her into a huge pile of mush.

'Okay. Can I offer you a piece of advice, Rhea?' Neha asked.

'Yeah, of course,' Rhea answered.

'Ask him to make you meet his parents. You don't realize the importance of it now…but you need to be on friendly terms with his parents. If you do it later, say around the time you start talking about marriage, your comfort level will be at the minimal level. And how do you know whether his parents will like you or not? I mean, you're amazing, Rhea, but you can never foresee what his parents will think. You need to start laying the foundation now,' Neha explained. 'If you leave it to the last minute, it'll be an extremely weird situation. They need to meet you as the girl Saahil is serious about. And for your own comfort level, start talking to them on a regular basis.'

Rhea was just staring at her friend. 'How the hell do you know so much about all this stuff?'

Neha snorted, 'Trust me, I wish I didn't know about all this stuff. But, unfortunately, I heard something recently and it's still pretty fresh in my brain, so I thought I'd tell you about it. A friend of mine had been dating this guy for a couple of years. I think around three to four years. That's a pretty long time, right? Both of them seemed perfectly compatible and perfect in every way. However, that boy never introduced her as his girlfriend to his parents. When she brought up marriage, he kept on saying that they will get married eventually, and to just be patient. Eventually, they both ended up breaking up, and my friend is beyond distraught.'

Rhea felt her heart sink. She had never put her mind to this stuff, and actually hearing it out loud was making it all too real.

'I don't mean to scare you, Rhea,' Neha said quickly, upon seeing Rhea's expression. 'I want to be a good friend and offer you the same sound advice, like how you told me to stand up for myself and talk to Karan when he was being an asshole. Just…think about it.'

Rhea nodded. Neha was right.

She'd been putting it off for far too long. The awkward conversation with Saahil needed to happen as soon as possible. The story she'd just heard had made shit real.

Rhea could feel the familiar impulsive feeling engulfing her.

She had to do something about this predicament. She checked the time on her phone. It was 8.00 p.m.

Saahil would be done with work by now.

She called him quickly, 'Hi. Want to meet for dinner? Okay, cool. See you soon.'

twenty-two

Saahil was in the middle of changing out of his work clothes when there was a knock on his bedroom door. 'One second!'

He quickly put on his most comfortable *Rolling Stones* T-shirt and cut-off shorts, and opened the door.

It was Rhea.

Saahil's face broke out in a smile as he motioned for her to enter. 'I didn't know it was you, sweetheart. I would have let you see me change otherwise.'

'You're funny. Is there no one at home? I can normally hear some TV blaring whenever I come, but tonight there is nothing,' Rhea said.

Saahil was momentarily distracted by her appearance. Even though she was dressed in work pants and a shirt, Rhea still managed to look exceptionally hot.

He walked over to her and pulled her close. He murmured, 'How do you manage to look so good even in work clothes?'

Before Rhea could answer, Saahil bent his head and covered her lips with his. He deepened the kiss when he heard her sigh and relax against him. It seemed like several minutes had passed before Rhea's hand came up his chest and gently pushed him away.

'How do you always manage to distract me? I was asking you something,' she whispered.

'Asking me what?' Saahil had moved on to kissing her neck.

Rhea laughed, 'I was asking whether anyone is at home

or not. And if someone is at home, you're being awfully brave by making out with your girlfriend with the door unlocked!'

Saahil finally let go of her and said, 'No one is at home. They all had some wedding function to attend. Dadi tried to force me to make an appearance, but I held my ground.'

However, Rhea only sighed and scrunched up her face.

'Rhea? What's wrong? You don't seem okay,' Saahil asked in a concerned voice.

On closer look, Saahil observed that Rhea looked slightly worried about something. Her smile didn't reach up to her eyes and she was unusually fidgety.

'Nope, everything's fine,' Rhea exclaimed. 'What are we eating? I'm starving.'

Saahil decided to not push her at the moment. He knew from past experience that Rhea would tell him what was troubling her before the night ended. She just needed time to gather her thoughts.

'Well, I thought we could have some Indian food,' Saahil announced.

Rhea snorted, 'Um, Saahil. Are you forgetting that you don't know how to eat Indian food?'

'Yeah, well, I know you love Indian food and I want to eat some with you. Under your supervision, I'm sure I'll manage,' Saahil said smilingly. 'How does rajma chawal sound? That's pretty basic, right? All you have to do is mix the rajma with the chawal and you're done. The cook here makes it really well so I thought we could have home food for a change.'

Rhea sighed and laughed at the same time. 'That sounds great, Saahil. I just can't believe that you don't know how to eat Indian food. You do know you've lived in India your entire life, right? You can't live in a country and not eat its food. That's just wrong.'

Rhea started pacing across the room and continued talking, 'I can list out so many things that don't make sense. You owe it to India to eat Indian food, Saahil. And I'm so mad at you.'

There it is.

Seemed like Rhea was going to tell him what was troubling her before the night ended, after all. Her rant about Indian food had been pretty hilarious, though.

'Why are you mad at me?' Saahil asked tenderly.

She looked so troubled that Saahil wanted to smile.

'Saahil, I want to meet your parents,' she announced quickly.

Okay, he had not been expecting that.

'Uh...what? Why would you want to do that, Rhea?' Saahil asked. This was so out of the blue that Saahil didn't know how to react.

It was his turn to pace around the room, while Rhea now stood silently next to the bed.

'I want to know more about your family. We've been together for almost two years and you've never made me meet them. I want to know more about my boyfriend's life. Is that so unfair?' Rhea asked quietly.

Saahil sighed, 'No. No, it's not.'

He knew she was right. He'd been dreading this meeting for a very long time.

He continued, 'Rhea...my parents are very different. They are poles apart from your mother, trust me on that. I don't know what your reaction will be when you meet them.'

'Saahil, why think of the worst even before it's happened? And I'm sure most of it is in your head,' Rhea assured him.

Saahil snorted. He so wished that was true.

'You keep your home life so separate from me. I've never said anything earlier, but…I want to know more about your life, Saahil,' Rhea continued.

Saahil lay down on his bed and tried to control his exasperation. He didn't know how to explain to her that meeting his parents was definitely going to open up a can of worms, and Saahil didn't want to deal with that.

'Wasn't Aunty in the fashion industry as well? I'm sure we could bond over that! What else does she like to do?' Rhea asked brightly.

That was certainly an interesting question.

Saahil shut his eyes for a second and let the memories flood through his mind.

∞

Saahil rang the doorbell to his mother's Pune apartment and waited for someone to open the door.

He was leaving for London in a week, and had come to say goodbye to Mom.

After waiting for a couple of minutes, the housekeeper finally opened the door and Saahil noticed that she looked scared.

'Mom kaha pe hai (Where is mom)?' Saahil asked.

She motioned toward his mother's bedroom and didn't say anything.

'Kya hua (What happened)?' Saahil prompted.

The housekeeper merely shook her head and motioned for Saahil to head on inside.

Saahil gave her a questioning look and knocked on his mother's door. When he didn't hear a reply, Saahil quietly opened it and looked inside.

The room was empty, but Saahil was greeted with the faint smell of alcohol as soon as he headed in.

The bathroom door was wide open, and Saahil could hear some music playing.

He inched closer, and what he saw next, almost stopped his heartbeat.

Payal was lying face down on the bathroom floor, with a bottle of vodka next to her.

Saahil acted on instinct. He felt his mind go numb as he tried to shake her. 'Mom. Mom. Get up.'

Payal mumbled something under her breath, but made no attempt to get up from the bathroom floor.

Kishore Kumar was blaring on her phone, and Saahil quickly shut it. He couldn't function with that music in the background.

He set the vodka bottle on the sink and bent down to pick up his mother.

Payal was so drunk that her body's normal weight had converted into dead weight. It was twice as difficult to lift her.

Saahil finally managed to get her in a sitting position and made her lean against the bathroom wall. Saahil took some water in a cup and splashed it on her face.

'Oh my God! What's going on?' Payal's eyes opened and she looked at him blinkingly.

'Mom. It's me, Saahil,' he said with no emotion in his voice.

'Saahil! Beta, I'm so happy you're here!' Payal leaned forward to hug him but instead ended up falling sideways to the floor again.

'Jeez, Mom, get a grip over yourself,' Saahil said. He made her lean against the wall again.

Saahil grabbed a bottle of water kept next to her bed and proceeded to make his mother drink it.

'Saahil, what are you doing here? Why aren't you in London? Are you done with college?' Payal slurred.

'I'm still in undergrad college, Mom. I leave next week. I told you that,' Saahil said quietly.

'Bed. I want to lie down on the bed,' Payal mumbled.

Finally, she was speaking some sense.

Saahil managed to make her stand, and used his arm to support her while walking forward. Payal rested her head on his shoulder as they took a step forward.

'Saahil. That man ruined my life, Saahil...'

Great, thought Saahil. They'd moved on to regular conversation now.

'Saahil, can I give you a piece of advice?' Payal asked.

Saahil nodded. It's not like he had the option of saying no.

'Don't ever get married, beta. Marriage is the worst thing ever,' Payal laughed as she got on to the bed.

And then it was lights out of her.

∞

'Saahil? Are you even listening to me?' Rhea asked with her brow furrowed.

Saahil noticed that she was sitting next to him on the bed as he jolted out of his thoughts.

'I was asking what does your mother like to do other than something related to fashion?' Rhea prompted again.

'Well... She likes to drink,' Saahil answered bluntly.

Rhea was taken aback for a second before saying, 'Oh. Okay. There's nothing wrong with that, of course.'

Saahil nodded.

'Saahil...it would mean a lot to me if I met them. I know that you're apprehensive about this, but trust me, it won't be too bad. And who knows? Maybe I'll end up loving your parents even more than I love you. Okay, I'm kidding. That's a long shot, but you get the gist. Besides, I did meet your Dad once, remember? When I was right outside your apartment? Not that we spoke, of course', Rhea commented.

Saahil nodded again. That had been some scene as well.

'Wait. They do know about me, right?' Rhea asked suddenly.

Saahil looked at Rhea and almost laughed. She looked so nervous and horrified.

'Yes, they know about you, Rhea. They know we've been dating since London. In fact, Mom has even mentioned a couple of times that she would like to meet you, but I've been putting it off. Maybe because I didn't know whether you would like to meet them. But, now that you've brought it up...'

Rhea swatted his arm, 'Saahil! I can't believe you. Why haven't you told me this earlier? God, I'm so mad at you.'

Saahil forced himself to smile at Rhea. He didn't stand a chance against those wide eyes and hopeful face.

He'd known that he'd have to make her meet them at some point, anyway. Might as well do it now.

'I'm sorry, Rhea,' Saahil apologized. 'But, yes, okay. Let's do it. Let's meet my parents.'

Upon seeing Rhea's wide smile, Saahil added, 'Besides, it should be interesting—it's been a long time since my parents have been in the same room together.'

'Oh, we're going to meet them together? I thought I can meet them individually,' Rhea said.

'No, I'd rather make you meet them together. If Mom found out that you're meeting Dad separately, she'll go on a whole different tangent—like how maybe you spoke to him more than her, and maybe you enjoyed meeting with him much more and all sorts of other nonsense. And Dad will be the same. They'll both analyse it to a great extent. Now, all I have to do is convince the both of them to meet you together. That's going to be quite a task,' Saahil explained with a short laugh.

'Okay, as you say. You're the boss,' Rhea said happily.

'Yes, I am. Now, how about that rajma chawal? I'm famished!' Saahil exclaimed.

twenty-three

'Relax, Rhea,' Saahil said.

They were in the car heading to Wasabi for dinner with Saahil's parents.

Rhea took a deep breath and looked at the pale pink floor-length dress she'd chosen to wear.

While deciding what to wear, Rhea had sought out Saahil's help. She was under the impression that she should wear some form of conservative Indian clothing, but Saahil had laughed his head off when he'd heard her.

Thus, the dress had won.

'I'm fine. Are we late? I hope we aren't late,' Rhea exclaimed in a panicked voice.

'We are literally two minutes away, and no, we are not late,' Saahil replied. He swerved the car to the left and slightly increased the pace of the car.

Rhea noticed his strained voice and tried to calm herself down. She knew she was putting Saahil on edge as well.

Finally, they reached their destination and Rhea waited on the porch of the Taj Mahal Hotel while Saahil handed his car keys to the valet.

She gave him a small smile as they headed to the restaurant. 'Thanks, Saahil. For this!'

Saahil laughed, 'I hope it's everything you're hoping it to be. Just...don't react a lot. That's my only piece of advice.'

Before Rhea could analyse Saahil's statement further, they

entered the restaurant and were immediately greeted by the restaurant manager. 'Welcome back, sir. We've given you the table in our most private area so that you won't be disturbed. Mrs Kapoor is already at the table,' he said with a smile.

Rhea felt her heart skip a beat.

Saahil guided her forward with his hand on the small of her back. They finally reached their table and Rhea was taken aback momentarily.

Saahil's mother was extremely beautiful. In her quick inspection, Rhea observed that she looked incredibly chic in her simple satin top and pants. While the outfit was very basic, she carried herself in such a way that it came across as equally formal.

'There you two are! Hello, Rhea beta! How are you?' Payal enveloped Rhea in a hug.

Rhea smiled, 'I'm fine, Aunty. It's so nice to finally meet you!'

'Same here, dear. I've been telling Saahil to make us meet for a while now, but I don't know what to do with this boy!' Payal gave Saahil a withering look as they sat down.

'Mom, chill,' Saahil stated.

Rhea observed that he had somewhat relaxed as well.

There was an open bottle of red wine on the table and the waiter suddenly appeared to refill Payal's glass. 'Should we order some more drinks? What are the two of you having?' she asked Saahil and Rhea.

'Shouldn't we wait for Uncle?' Rhea asked.

She saw Payal's expression change. 'That man is never on time, Rhea. You might as well order something. We'll all be waiting a long time for him,' she informed.

On closer look, Rhea saw that there were fine lines etched

across Payal's face. You can't see them from a distance but are unmissable on a closer look.

Payal looked slightly haggard because of them.

'Mom,' Saahil said quietly.

'What? You know it's true!' Payal said innocently.

Suddenly, there was a loud noise of someone talking on the phone and Rhea saw Saahil's father walking toward the table. He was talking heatedly over the phone and was visibly annoyed at whatever the other person was saying.

Finally, he reached his destination and said over the phone, 'Okay, I've reached. I'll call you once I'm done. Yes. Me too. Bye.'

'Rhea. Nice to meet you,' Manan shook Rhea's hand before sitting across from his former wife.

'Nice to meet you too, Uncle,' Rhea smiled.

Okay, the temperature at the table is beyond frosty now, Rhea observed.

'Payal,' Manan nodded at his ex-wife. This was their greeting after all these years.

'Hello, Manan. I was just telling the kids that they shouldn't wait for you to order their drinks. Being late is your speciality, isn't it?' Payal smiled sarcastically at him.

Rhea heard Saahil exhale sharply. Thankfully, Manan remained silent and ignored Payal's snide comment.

'So. Rhea. It's nice to finally meet you properly,' Manan said to Rhea.

'Likewise, Uncle,' Rhea replied.

'Rhea, I take it you're in the fashion field?' Payal interrupted.

'Yes. I'm working under Sukhvinder Rajput's brand currently,' Rhea explained.

'Wow, that's amazing. I was in the fashion field myself before it was all taken away from me,' Payal said.

'Should we place the appetizers order?' Saahil cut in.

'What do you mean by that?' Manan asked her. 'It wasn't taken away from you. You left it to rot when you stopped paying attention to it.'

'And why did I stop paying attention to it, Manan?' Payal shot back.

'Guys,' Saahil said loudly. 'I'm placing the order. Mom, vegetarian for you, right?'

'Yes,' Payal sniffed. She realized her wine glass was empty and motioned for the waiter to refill it. 'Aren't you ordering something to drink, Saahil? And what about you, Rhea?'

'I'm good, Aunty. I'll stick with water,' Rhea replied quickly.

'Same here,' Saahil said.

Both Payal and Manan gave Saahil a surprised look. Rhea had to fight really hard to control her chuckle.

Well done, Saahil.

Saahil quickly placed the appetizers order, and Rhea saw him give her a sideways glance.

She smiled at him quickly, showing that she was fine.

'What are your future plans, Rhea? Do you plan on working under this brand long term?' Manan asked Rhea.

'Honestly, I don't know. I might branch out on my own,' Rhea admitted.

It was the first time she'd ever put her thoughts to words and it felt good.

'That's very good. I like that attitude. You'll do wonders if you're ambitious from a young age,' Manan smiled. His phone rang and he put it on silent.

'Manan, you can pick up your girlfriend's call. We won't mind,' Payal commented.

No one said anything.

'Oh, please. We all know it's her calling. Rhea, whenever his phone used to ring at the dinner table, I knew it was a girl calling,' Payal laughed.

Rhea noticed that the bottle of wine was almost empty and Payal's eyes were slightly glazed over.

She decided it was best to remain silent and not comment.

'Tell me, Rhea, what would you do if Saahil kept on getting calls at the dinner table?' Payal prompted.

Uh…what?

'Mom. That's enough,' Saahil said quietly. His eyes were dead serious and Rhea saw him clench his fingers around the glass of water.

'Okay. Okay. I'm sorry,' Payal threw up her hands. 'Let's talk about something else. How long have you two been dating now?'

'Around a year and a half,' Rhea replied.

'That's a long time. I've never seen Saahil in a relationship that long,' Manan commented.

'How would you? He is ultimately his father's son, isn't he?' Payal laughed harshly. 'You set such a bad example for our son.'

Oh, fuck.

There was silence on the table again. Saahil's knuckles had turned white while holding the glass.

'Payal,' Manan finally spoke. 'Drop it.'

'Why should I drop it? All you ever wanted me to do was drop it, Manan!' Payal cried in anguish.

Rhea saw Saahil's father look at him helplessly. Saahil shrugged in response.

Rhea didn't blame him. If she was feeling this odd, she couldn't even imagine what Saahil was going through.

Finally, the appetizers arrived, and Rhea heard Saahil breathe a sigh of relief. She wanted to squeeze his hand under the table, but knew it would be highly inappropriate.

Not that anything going on at the table was appropriate.

'Saahil, please order another bottle of wine for me,' Payal instructed.

'Mom, I think you should eat something first,' Saahil replied.

'Yes, Payal. Eat something,' Manan chipped in.

Payal laughed heartily at his statement. 'Now, coming from you, that's truly ironic. How many times did you used to fall asleep without having any food and only a bottle of whiskey in your system? Please, don't tell me what to do, Manan. You're the last one to do that.'

Manan sighed and motioned for the waiter to come to the table, 'Another bottle of wine, please.'

Payal turned to Rhea, 'A word of friendly advice, Rhea. Don't ever take shit from men. They walk all over you and leave you to gather the pieces.'

Manan turned to look at Rhea as well, 'And, Rhea, make sure you always hold yourself responsible for what might be your mistake. Women tend to play the damsel in distress card one too many a times and put the blame on someone else entirely. While you may get away with once or twice, it's important to stop before it becomes a habit.'

'Oh, really? Are you calling me a damsel in distress?' Payal asked Manan sharply.

'I wasn't speaking to you, Payal,' Manan replied.

'Well, you might as well be,' Payal shot back. 'You're back to your dirty tricks, Manan.'

Manan's phone rang again.

Saahil suddenly got up abruptly. 'Okay, I've tolerated this bullshit long enough. Mom, eat something before you make a fool out of yourself. Dad, pick up your phone and talk to your girlfriend. If I hear another word of nonsense at this table, I'm taking Rhea and walking out!'

twenty-four

Rhea and Saahil barely spoke a word on the way back from the restaurant.

Some old Bollywood song was blaring from the radio, but Rhea couldn't even fire up her brain enough to recognize the song.

She didn't know what to think about.

After Saahil's sudden outburst, his parents had fallen silent. In some weird sadistic sense, Rhea felt that the dinner atmosphere had been better when they were snapping at each other. At least, there had been some noise at the table.

The four of them had finished dinner as quickly as possible, and left.

Saahil's mother had been gracious enough to invite Rhea to dinner again next week, and before she could respond, Saahil's father had jumped in with his own dinner invite as well.

She had ended up accepting both invites.

'So,' Rhea said brightly. 'Are you hungry?'

Rhea wanted to lighten the mood. Saahil looked so solemn that she wanted to say something to make him smile.

'Huh? Sorry, what did you say?' Saahil asked. She seemed to have disturbed his thoughts.

'I said…are you hungry?' Rhea asked again.

'Now that I think about it, I'm quite hungry. I barely ate anything,' Saahil said after a pause.

'Yes, I noticed that. Do you want to go to my place? Mom

isn't in town—she's on some business trip. I can make a grilled cheese sandwich. That's the extent of my gourmet cooking,' Rhea said smilingly.

Saahil smiled as well, 'That sounds amazing. Home it is.'

They reached her building within the next fifteen minutes, and Rhea removed her high heels as soon as they entered the apartment.

'Oh my God,' Rhea groaned. 'That feels so good.'

Saahil didn't say anything. She noticed that he'd sat on the living room couch and was staring off into space.

Rhea felt her heart melt. He didn't deserve this.

'Saahil,' Rhea said softly as she sat next to him. 'Stop thinking about it.'

Saahil jumped slightly at her words. 'Stop thinking about what?'

'Dinner,' Rhea said.

'Oh, please,' Saahil scoffed. 'I'm not thinking about that. I was just thinking about something related to the app.'

'Oh, okay. I can play along if that's what you want,' Rhea smiled. She stroked his hair and planted a kiss on his forehead.

'Your mother is so beautiful, Saahil,' Rhea continued. She got up and turned on the television.

'What about my grilled cheese?' Saahil ignored her statement as she came back to the couch.

'In a bit. My feet hurt,' Rhea complained.

Saahil brought her feet over to his lap and started kneading them with his knuckles.

Rhea groaned loudly again.

Saahil laughed, 'Now, *that's* a sound I like my woman to make.'

'Shut up,' Rhea closed her eyes and felt herself relax.

'Saahil, I know you don't want to talk about it. But, I do,' Rhea said. When he didn't say anything, Rhea continued with her eyes closed, 'Have they always been like this?'

'As far back as I can remember, yes,' Saahil said quietly.

'They have a lot of animosity for each other,' Rhea commented.

'Yes, they do,' he agreed.

'But, I guess, all married couples must have some level of animosity for each other. Some more than others, of course,' Rhea said quickly as she opened her eyes and saw Saahil staring at her. 'Living with each other all the time must get on your nerves.'

'Rhea,' Saahil said. 'You don't need to defend my parents. Their relationship is screwed up and they certainly weren't like most married couples when they were together.'

'I guess,' Rhea said. She removed her feet from Saahil's lap and sat up straight. 'But, I'm trying to say that all married couples must have some issue or the other to deal with.'

'Maybe,' Saahil commented.

'I really hope that doesn't happen to us, you know. I guess it's inevitable to fall into the married-couple rut, but I hope our marriage doesn't fall into the clichéd category. It's so crazy to think that people who love each other so much can end up hurting each other the most at times. It's something to think about, isn't it?' Rhea asked.

She'd meant it to be a rhetorical question, but when she looked over at him, Saahil looked like he'd just seen a ghost.

'Saahil? What's wrong? You've turned white!' Rhea exclaimed.

'What did you just say?' Saahil asked quietly. His voice had no expression in it.

No expression or emotion at all.

'I was...just talking about how marriages fall into a rut. And I hope that doesn't happen to our married life,' Rhea repeated.

Rhea was confused. Why was he making a big deal out of this?

'Our marriage?' Saahil said. 'Rhea, what do you mean by that? You know I can't get married, right?'

Rhea was taken aback for a second, but quickly composed herself, 'Saahil, obviously I don't mean right now. I don't want to get married right now as well. I meant that *eventually* when we do get married, I hope we're different.'

'Rhea,' Saahil said. 'Just hold on for a second. Let me rephrase that. I *won't* ever get married. I *don't* ever want to get married. And I'm not just saying this because of tonight's drama—I've always known this about myself.'

Rhea was speechless. She didn't know what to say next.

Her heart was closing up, and she tried to take deep breaths.

She got up from the couch, and looked at Saahil. He was still the same white colour as he'd been earlier.

'You don't want to get married?' Rhea whispered. 'Ever?'

Saahil tried to grab Rhea's hand, but she took her hand away.

She needed her distance from him to completely understand what he was saying.

'Rhea,' Saahil said quietly. 'You saw my parents tonight. They screwed up each other's life once they got married. Not just them, but most people screw up everything after marriage. How many times have you heard of people having extra-marital affairs? Hell, my own father slept with half the city of Mumbai when he was married to my mother. You saw my mother's state tonight. This is what her marriage did to her. Okay, forget cheating. You said so yourself earlier—how married couples end up hurting each other. Well, Rhea, I saw first-hand how miserable my parents made each other. Why would you want to enter this fucked-up institution where all people do is fuck up each other's happiness?'

Rhea felt numb inside. She managed to whisper, 'It's not everyone, Saahil. Everyone is different. Doesn't mean that the same thing has to happen to you as well.'

Saahil got up as well. 'Rhea, I can't take that chance.'

'Can't? Or won't?' Rhea said softly.

Saahil threw up his hands. 'Okay, I won't take that chance. You heard my mother tonight. I am my father's son at the end of the day, right? I will sabotage my own relationships. The apple doesn't fall far from the tree. And it's not just my father, Rhea. My mother had her own affair in the marriage, which ultimately led to my father having innumerable affairs. Both my parents have fucked up, and, eventually, I will fuck up as well. I just don't want to put you in that position.'

Rhea felt tears rolling down her cheeks. She was taking in whatever Saahil was saying, but couldn't say anything.

Saahil gave a short laugh, 'Rhea, you may think that everything that I'm saying is so superficial. But, trust me, I have lived through it and it's the most unpleasant situation in the world. I don't want to put you in that situation. Ever. I don't trust myself, Rhea. I just don't. I've seen how fucked up my world is, and I don't want you to enter it.'

'Isn't that my decision?' Rhea sobbed. She saw Saahil take a step toward her but held up a hand to stop him. 'Just… please don't come near. I need to think.'

'What's there to think about? I love you. I love you so much. Before I met you, I didn't think that I could be a serious boyfriend to anyone. But you proved me wrong, Rhea. Stuff is go good between us—why do we need to bring up marriage?' Saahil cried in anguish.

'I wasn't bringing up marriage. I was talking about a hypothetical situation far off in the future, Saahil,' Rhea said through her tears. She suddenly laughed, 'God, I'm so dumb! To think that I wanted to meet my boyfriend's parents so that eventually when we do get married, we're comfortable with each other and not strangers. But, little did I know that my boyfriend doesn't even want to get married. And you know what? I'm even dumber to not have brought up marriage all this time. I mean, I always thought that down the line, it was going to happen for us. But did I even think to talk to my boyfriend of almost two years about it? No, I didn't. Fuck! How could I just presume? How could I have been so stupid?'

'Rhea,' Saahil shook his head. 'Just stop. Listen to me. I recently found out that my father's cheating on his current girlfriend as well. I walked in on them at Café Prato. When I confronted him about it, he made me realize that I'm no one to preach. I don't have a great track record myself. Being a boyfriend to you is one thing. A husband—that means committing to each other for life. I don't know how I will be as a husband, Rhea! I don't have good examples in front of me. What if I cheat on you? What if I cheat on you more than once? What if I come home drunk out of my head, not knowing where I've been the entire night? I don't want to lie to you. And, eventually, in order to cover my tracks, I will have to lie to you. Do you want that, Rhea?'

'No, of course, I don't!' Rhea suddenly shouted. 'Saahil,

why the fuck are you comparing yourself to your parents? You're so much more than that. You've come so far. You've made so much progress. You're not them, Saahil—why don't you get that?'

'Because they're a part of me, Rhea! I *am* their son,' Saahil shouted. 'Just because you have the most amazing mother in the world, doesn't mean we're all blessed with the same privilege!'

Rhea felt stung. She didn't know how to respond.

Saahil rubbed his face with his hands. 'I'm sorry. I didn't mean that, Rhea,' he said as he took step toward her. 'Why don't we forget this entire conversation? How did we start talking about this in the first place? I love you. Let's just forget it all, please.'

'Saahil,' Rhea said quietly. 'I want you to leave. Right now. I need to be by myself.'

'What? Rhea, please. Let's just forget this entire topic and go back to the way we were!' Saahil exclaimed.

Rhea felt the tears roll down her cheeks again and shook her head.

'Rhea,' Saahil said urgently. He finally came closer and wrapped his arms around her waist. 'Please, Rhea. Stop this. Let's forget it, please.'

His embrace felt so familiar that Rhea couldn't help resting her head on his chest and letting the tears fall.

As much as her heart was saying something else, her mind had already been made up, and she couldn't ignore it.

She knew how headstrong Saahil could be, and that there was no way he was going to change his mind about marriage.

Rhea cupped her hand over his cheek and whispered, 'I can't believe I'm saying this...but I'm sorry, Saahil. I want more. I can't help it. I do want to get married, eventually. Its just want I want. I'm trying to picture myself in the future, and I do want that happy ending.'

She saw that Saahil was about to speak so she held up a hand to stop him. 'Just let me finish, please. And if you know me, you know that I need to say it. I can't pretend to live in denial. If I don't say it now…I might not have the courage later.'

Saahil took a step back from her. His face was closed up, but when Rhea saw his eyes, she wanted to cry all over again.

Just a few more minutes. Just a few more minutes and then she could curl up on the couch and cry her heart out.

She took a deep breath before speaking in a clear voice, 'I know you're going to think that I'm making this decision without thinking it through. I love you so much, Saahil. I can't believe that I'm doing this. But…I can't help it. I want more—I don't want to compromise on what I know will make me happy. I can't overlook the fact that you never want to get married. There's no point of us being together if we want different things. As much as I love you. I'm sorry.'

twenty-five

Eight Months Later

'Can we have the crispy okra, chicken lollipop and ghee-roast mutton?' Rhea said to the server at Farzi Café. She'd heard that these were the must-try items on the menu.

'Sure, ma'am. Anything to drink with that?' the waiter asked.

'I'm good, thanks.' She looked over to her companion and asked, 'Kunaal, what about you?'

'Hmm?' Kunaal looked up from his phone screen. 'I wouldn't mind a whiskey on the rocks.'

Saahil's drink.

Rhea quickly wiped that thought from her head, and focused her attention on her dinner date. 'Have you been to Farzi Café before?'

Kunaal smiled, 'Yes, I have. It's my favourite place to come for a late-night meal.'

Rhea looked around the restaurant and commented, 'It does have a cozy feel to it.'

'Yes, it does,' Kunaal said smilingly. 'How was work?'

'Work was…good. It's picking up. I'm still not sure whether I made the right decision by leaving Sukhvinder Rajput, but I'm finally doing what I want to. I'm exhibiting under my own brand in a couple of weeks, and it's a different kind of exhilaration!' Rhea exclaimed.

Kunaal laughed, 'Yes, I'm sure it is. I am so glad that you called today. I had a good time the last time we met for dinner.'

Rhea smiled back at him.

This was the third time she was meeting Kunaal. They'd met at a common friend's party initially and had ended up talking for a while. Rhea had found him sweet, a good conversationalist and definitely not hard on the eyes.

'I'm glad we did this again, too. I heard someone talk about how good Farzi Café is, and I felt like I should definitely try it out now,' Rhea said.

'There are so many small food joints in Mumbai that are amazing. Some of them are even better than those upscale fine-dining restaurants. Have you ever tried Tibbs Frankie?' Kunaal asked.

The waiter came over with Kunaal's drink, and set it on the table. 'Your food is on the way. Enjoy.'

'Nope. Never been,' Rhea replied.

'Dude, Rhea, you're missing out on life. They're to die for,' Kunaal said excitedly.

Rhea felt like laughing seeing how excited he was about food.

'I take it you're a foodie,' she commented.

'Oh, yes. I love food. It's my favourite thing to talk about. If I hadn't been forced to be a part of my father's marketing firm, I would have been a chef,' Kunaal said.

Just like Saahil. Forced to do something he didn't want to.

Rhea shook her head. Why the hell did he pop into her head at the weirdest of times?

'Why were you forced? Did you tell him what you want to do?' Rhea enquired.

'There was no point in that. I'd been told from the very beginning that as soon as I'm done with college, I have to join my father's business. I knew there's no point of debate on this topic, so I didn't even bother,' Kunaal explained.

Rhea nodded. It was frustrating the way Indian families functioned.

'How's your mother doing? I don't think I know anyone who's seen as many movies as her!' Kunaal stated.

Rhea laughed. The last time they'd met for dinner, he'd come to pick up Rhea at home. Her mother had, of course, spoken to Kunaal at length before they'd left the apartment. They'd discussed everything ranging from movies to food to work.

Simran Singh certainly approved of Kunaal.

Ever since Rhea and Saahil had broken up, her mother had been extra protective. While it was sweet, it was also highly unnecessary. It's not like every guy was going to be the same roller coaster ride that Saahil had been.

'I like roller coasters, though,' Rhea muttered under her breath.

'I'm sorry? I didn't catch that,' Kunaal said.

'Oh, nothing. I was just saying that Mom and I love watching all sorts of movies. It's one of our favourite pastimes. We recently watched the new *Mowgli*, and it was so good,' Rhea said quickly.

'Oh, yes, I loved that movie. There are so many good movies that have come out recently. Are you fond of Bollywood movies at all or no?' Kunaal asked.

Rhea noticed that he was looking at her extremely closely. It made her feel uncomfortable.

She dropped her gaze quickly and replied, 'I'm not very

fond of them, to be honest. It depends on the story line. For example, I loved *PK*. That was a fantastic movie.'

Kunaal laughed, 'Yes, Aamir Khan was spectacular in it. He's such an amazing actor.'

Rhea saw from the corner of her eye that the food had arrived, and felt her stomach grumble. She realized that she'd not eaten anything the entire day. Work had been crazy, and she'd just not gotten the time to grab a bite.

The waiter began piling the food on the table and Rhea felt her thoughts wander.

She knew she'd taken a big risk by leaving her previous job, especially since the salary they'd been offering her had been pretty great. But, the level of satisfaction that Rhea got from working for her own brand made her feel ten times more accomplished.

She sighed. There was a long way to go.

'What's wrong, Rhea?' Kunaal asked in a concerned voice.

'Nothing's wrong,' Rhea said with a flick of her hand. 'I was just thinking about work.'

'Just leave all thoughts related to work aside for a few minutes and concentrate on this roast mutton. It's out of this world,' Kunaal said with his mouth full.

Rhea laughed. His enthusiasm for food was infectious.

Kunaal was right. Everything, including the mutton, was incredible.

By the time Rhea was done eating, she was ready to pass out.

'There's just something about Indian food,' Rhea said as she wiped her hands on the tablecloth. 'It makes you want to pass out on the bed as soon as you're done.'

Kunaal laughed, 'You're right. I'm just about ready to burst.'

They decided to call for the cheque with unanimous agreement, and quickly headed to Kunaal's car after paying.

When they were about to reach her building, Rhea felt Kunaal put his hand on top of hers. 'I had a really good time tonight, Rhea.'

Shit.

She didn't say anything but merely smiled when she saw Kunaal looking over at her.

'Do you think we can do this again soon?' He asked.

Rhea took a deep breath and answered, 'Sure.'

The car finally pulled up beneath Rhea's building and she let out a small sigh of relief. They were within her comfort territory again.

There was silence in the car.

Just as she was about to open the car door, Rhea felt Kunaal touch her arm. He was gazing at her deeply.

Oh, no.

She saw him lean toward her, his eyes now on her lips.

Kunaal quickly closed the distance between them and kissed her softly.

Several moments passed before he raised his head and looked at her.

Rhea felt like kicking herself.

She could have at least pretended to be slightly into the kiss.

It's not like Kunaal was a bad kisser.

She just…hadn't been into it.

'Well,' Kunaal began.

Rhea forced herself to smile, 'Yes. Well. Thanks for tonight. Goodnight…'

'Yes, goodnight, Rhea,' Kunaal said quickly.

He seemed to be in a hurry to leave.

Rhea waited till his car sped off before stepping into the elevator. She groaned when the doors shut.

That had been supremely awkward.

'You could have at least kissed him back, idiot,' she muttered to herself.

Poor guy.

As soon as she entered the apartment, she was greeted by a loud voice, 'How was it, beta? Did you have fun?'

'Mom?' Rhea looked at her mother quizzically. 'Why are you awake?'

'Well, I wanted to know how your date went, baby,' Simran replied enthusiastically.

'Ah,' Rhea commented.

'Well?'

She looked so excited to hear her reply that Rhea almost felt bad for breaking her bubble.

'It's not going to happen, Mom,' Rhea said dejectedly. 'I'm not going to see him again.'

'Huh? Why not?' Simran asked, confused.

'I'm just…not into him, I guess,' Rhea admitted. 'I don't feel that connect, you know?'

'That's such a shame,' Simran said sadly. 'That boy had such exquisite taste in food and movies.'

Rhea laughed loudly. 'We'll find you someone who you can talk about food and movies with, Mom. It's just not going to be Kunaal.'

'Oh, well,' Simran sighed. 'Are you sure about this, Rhea? He seemed like a really nice boy.'

Rhea sat down on the living room couch and curled up into her blanket. She sighed and closed her eyes before speaking, 'Yes, Mom. I'm sure.'

She felt a wave of sadness wash over her. It happened to her sometimes—everything would be fine and then suddenly... it just wasn't.

Several minutes passed, and Rhea felt her mother stroking her hair as she sat next to her.

'I miss him, Mom,' Rhea said softly.

She felt tears pricking her eyes.

'I know, beta,' Simran replied.

'Can I ask you something?' Rhea sniffled.

Fuck, the tears were falling now.

'Yes, beta. Anything,' Simran answered.

'Can we please get a dog?' Rhea sobbed.

twenty-six

'Saahil, beta? *Tum kahan pe ho* (Where are you)?' Dadi shouted over the phone.

Saahil jumped in his office chair. His grandmother's voice could jolt his senses at any given time.

'Dadi, I'm still at office. Anything urgent?' Saahil asked.

'Saahil! It's 9.00 p.m., come home right now! All these late hours at the office are becoming a nuisance! I want you home in ten minutes! You hear me, young man?' Dadi screamed and hung up.

What the hell?

Saahil had not been expecting that outburst.

He sighed and stretched his arms above his head. His grandmother was right, though.

Saahil had been running himself ragged over the past couple of months when it came to work, and he had no plans of stopping anytime soon.

His app venture was finally gaining some momentum, and he was also beginning to enjoy working at his father's steel company.

His stomach grumbled. He'd been stuck in meetings all day long and had forgotten to eat.

He decided to go back home.

Saahil called for his Range Rover to be brought to the porch and was soon on his way.

He tried to knock off the sunken feeling in his stomach.

The feeling of going home always left him with dread nowadays.

Life had only been about all work and no play for the last few months.

Saahil left for work early in the morning and returned home past 10.00 p.m. every day. He tried to work till the time he was so exhausted that all he could do when he reached home was pass out.

That certainly kept his thoughts at bay.

Even then, he hadn't slept properly for a couple of months now. His troubled sleeping patterns had been making an appearance much more frequently.

Saahil reached home within a matter of minutes, and saw that there were at least a dozen cars in his driveway.

He groaned. Had his grandparents kept a party of their crowd? He definitely didn't want to touch the feet of a million elderly people right now.

Saahil craned his neck to see inside the house, but all the lights were off.

That was strange.

If there was a party going on, why were all the lights off?

Saahil walked toward the front door and noticed that it was slightly ajar.

Crap. Something was definitely wrong now. He wished he had a baseball bat or something to carry over his head in case of a potential burglary.

As soon as Saahil stepped into the foyer, all the lights turned on and he blinked several times.

'Surprise!'

There were up to thirty of his friends gathered by the entrance of the house, holding balloons and banners that said 'Happy Birthday, Saahil!' His grandparents were in the centre holding a huge cake with smiles on their faces.

Shit.

Saahil had completely forgotten that it was his birthday tomorrow.

He really must have had the most bewildered expression on his face because everyone burst out laughing.

'Saahil, beta. Come,' Dada motioned Saahil towards him.

As the rest of his friends started mingling around while waiting for their turn to wish him, Saahil went to his grandparents and touched their feet.

Predictably, his father was nowhere to be seen.

'Thank you, Dada and Dadi. I…forgot it was my birthday tomorrow,' Saahil said sheepishly.

'We know, beta. You've been working too much. And no need to say thanks—we wish you all the happiness and success in the world,' Dadi said lovingly. 'Now, enjoy with your friends, and don't you dare wake up early tomorrow! We'll leave now, so that we don't embarrass you any further. And Saahil…please shave. You look like a gunda!'

With that statement, his grandparents bid him adieu and Saahil was left standing in the middle of the foyer. He rubbed his hand over his grown beard and sighed. Dadi was right—he hadn't shaved in weeks and his hair had grown out. He really did resemble a hooligan.

But, it definitely resembled his mood for the last—god knows how many days.

He looked around and noticed that it was most of his school friends that had gathered for his birthday celebrations.

'Saahil! Almost happy birthday, man!' Abhishek shouted as he clapped Saahil on the back. Abhishek was the first friend that Saahil had made in school, and they'd always had a special bond.

'Thanks, bro,' Saahil replied with a smile.

'Should we head to the living room? We've set up an entire bar there. All that was missing was your presence to kick off the celebrations!' Abhishek exclaimed.

Abhishek was right. His living room had been turned into a lounge of sorts.

After all his friends had taken turns wishing him, Saahil felt beyond exhausted. All he wanted to do was go up to his room and play FIFA.

'Saahil! What are you drinking, my man?' Deepak asked. He was also one of Saahil's classmates from school.

'Uh...to be very honest, nothing at all, bro. I'm really tired,' Saahil admitted.

Whoever was standing nearby, along with Deepak, turned to look at Saahil in shock.

'What? What's wrong?' Saahil asked, confused to see everyone staring at him.

'Saahil, are you feeling okay?' Abhishek asked in a concerned voice.

'Yes, why?' Saahil replied.

Someone had turned on the music and dimmed the lights. The party was picking up.

'Well, in all the years that I've known you, ever since we started drinking, you have never ever turned down alcohol. Thus, my concern over your mental state is quite appropriate,' Abhishek answered.

Saahil chuckled as he sat down on the nearest sofa. 'Nothing like that. I just have to get to work early tomorrow, that's all.'

It was true. Saahil had barely had alcohol ever since...

Well, ever since Rhea.

Saahil's mind went into overdrive as soon she entered his mind. He checked the time on his phone and it was a little over 10.00 p.m.

He wondered if Rhea would wish him on his birthday.

Saahil's throat clenched up. He was stupid to think that she would wish him.

All the times that Saahil had tried to contact her post the break-up, she had never responded. It was as if their entire relationship had gone up in smoke in an instant. Saahil wondered sometimes how easy it had been for her to block him out of her life.

But then again, Rhea Singh was extremely stubborn and strong when it came to things she really believed in.

'Hi, Saahil,' a voice said next to him. 'Mind if I sit down?'

Saahil looked over and saw that it was Kanika smiling at him. He observed that she'd changed a lot since school—Kanika could easily pass off as an actress now.

'Hey, Kanika,' Saahil replied. 'Yeah, of course. Can I fix you anything to drink?'

'Um…yeah, okay. A glass of red wine, please. But, Saahil, please have a drink as well. Come on. It's your birthday!' Kanika exclaimed as she sat down on the sofa.

Saahil thought for a moment before replying, 'Okay. I'll be right back.'

He walked over to the set up bar and poured some red wine into a glass, and made himself a drink consisting of vodka, soda, lime and salt. He got nostalgic whenever he had this drink—it reminded him of the night he and Rhea had smoked up together for the first time.

Whenever Saahil did drink now, he only had Rhea's favourite drink.

Saahil walked back toward Kanika and sat down next to her. 'Cheers.'

'Cheers,' she smiled as they clinked glasses. 'It's been so long since I've seen you, Saahil. Don't be such a stranger.'

Saahil smiled as well, 'Sorry. I've just been really caught up with work.'

'And your girlfriend, right?' Kanika asked with her eyebrows raised.

Her question caught him off guard. Rhea popped into his mind once again.

'Um, no. We broke up a while back,' Saahil said quietly.

'Oh,' Kanika commented. Her face brightened. 'I had no idea.'

'Yeah,' Saahil said.

When Saahil didn't say anything further, she continued, 'You know what, Saahil? You broke a lot of hearts when you finally started dating…what was her name? Anyway, doesn't matter. I know quite a few girls who wanted to kill her.'

Saahil wanted to walk away. She was obviously pretending to not know Rhea's name and it was pissing him off.

'Oh, really? I had no idea,' Saahil forced himself to say.

'Well, when all the girls heard that Saahil Kapoor was finally in a serious relationship, it was as if the Armageddon had dawned on this planet. It was always an unsaid challenge over who would finally be able to crack your no relationship rule!' Kanika laughed.

The music had picked up in the distance, and Saahil saw a couple of his friends take shots.

Just thinking about shots made his stomach queasy. He took a sip of his drink and turned back toward Kanika.

'That's quite…interesting to hear,' Saahil said.

He honestly had no interest what all the girls out there had been thinking.

And what was that crap about an unsaid challenge? What the fuck? These girls needed to get a life.

Kanika continued to talk for a couple of minutes, but Saahil had blocked her out. He merely nodded along to her words, but was secretly wondering whether he could go up to his room unnoticed.

Kanika must have sensed his boredom because she suddenly leaned forward.

Her low-cut dress displayed an ample amount of cleavage and she shoved it in front of under Saahil's face so that he could get the full view. She slid her hand above Saahil's knee and whispered, 'Okay, enough beating around the bush. Now that I know you're single and back to your old ways, I can finally say what I've always wanted to. What do you say we take this conversation somewhere…private? I would love to see your room.'

Saahil looked at her cleavage and then at her face.

Kanika really was drop dead gorgeous.

He almost laughed. A couple of years back, Saahil wouldn't have dreamt of saying no to a girl like her.

'Kanika, what makes you think that I'm back to my old ways?' Saahil asked.

Kanika slid her hand even upward. 'Well, aren't you?'

'I'm sorry,' Saahil said as he removed her hand from his thigh. 'But, I'm not.'

Kanika looked confused.

'I can't do this. I'm sorry,' Saahil said.

'What? Why not?' Kanika looked enraged that someone had said no to her advances.

Saahil stared at her for a second as he gathered his thoughts.

All he could he think about was Rhea.

Her eyes sparkling when she laughed...the feel of her hair against his fingers...how her lips tasted when he kissed her...

'Because...you're not her,' Saahil said simply, shaking his head. 'You're not Rhea.'

twenty-seven

Saahil tried to keep himself from jumping out of the chair and doing a victory dance.

'Saahil, things are looking very good. The company that I put you in touch with in Bangalore loved all your ideas for the app,' Saahil's tech liaison, Mr Kumar, announced.

'That's great, Mr Kumar,' Saahil said quietly.

He knew he couldn't look overtly excited or else he would come off as desperate.

'As we all know, Facebook has been surpassed by Instagram currently. It's time to make a change and remind people what Facebook was initially constructed for,' Mr Kumar continued.

'I couldn't agree more,' Saahil said.

'Congratulations, Saahil. I'll keep you posted about any progress and when you'll need to fly down to Bangalore to hash out further details,' Mr Kumar said as he shook Saahil's hand.

As soon as his associate had left the Oberoi Hotel coffee shop, Saahil pumped his fist in the air.

Yes! Finally!

All the months of brainstorming to make the app attractive and user-friendly had finally paid off. This was going to be the start of something big hopefully.

Saahil shook his head. He needed to calm down.

This was just the beginning and the road ahead was going to be filled with more hard work and hurdles.

Saahil picked up his phone and typed in Rhea's number.

Just as he was about to press the call icon, he caught himself.

What the fuck was he doing?

Rhea. He wanted to call her and tell her the good news.

She was the only person who he wanted to share the news with.

Fuck.

Saahil rubbed his hand over his face and leaned back into his seat. He couldn't believe he'd almost called her.

Feeling the high of his victory starting to wear off, Saahil got up and picked up his laptop bag.

Just as he was about to leave, he felt someone call out his name. 'Saahil?'

Saahil turned around and almost bumped into Nandini.

Oh, crap.

'Oh, hi, Nandini. How are you?' Saahil asked.

'I'm good, Saahil. What about you?' Nandini asked smilingly. She looked every bit the businesswoman in her black blazer and pants.

'Good as well,' Saahil replied.

There was silence after that. The awkward pleasantries were done and over with.

'Did you just get here?' Saahil asked.

'Yes. Just waiting for someone,' she answered.

'Oh. Is Dad coming here?' Saahil looked around to see if his father was in the nearby vicinity.

A strange look came over Nandini's face. 'Why would your father be joining, Saahil? Do you not know?'

'Know what?' Saahil asked, confused.

Nandini gave a short laugh. 'Wow. Communication really sucks in your household, huh? Your father and I broke up four months ago.'

Huh? This is news.

'What? Shit. I had no idea, Nandini,' Saahil said with a baffled expression.

Nandini hesitated for a minute before saying, 'Saahil, are you in a hurry? If you don't mind…can we have a cup of coffee? The person I'm meeting isn't going to be here for a bit, anyway.'

Saahil couldn't see a way out of this. He gave in to the inevitable and motioned for her to sit at the table.

'Thanks,' Nandini smiled.

Saahil quickly placed an order for two cappuccinos and sat across Nandini.

When she didn't say anything, Saahil asked curiously, 'So, why did you two break-up? I was under the impression that things were going really well?'

Nandini scoffed, 'Well, they were, till I found out what a cheating asshole your father is. No offence.'

Saahil snorted, 'None taken. I hope you don't find it odd that I didn't know about the breakup. My father and I have barely exchanged a word other than work for a very long time now. And I prefer it this way.'

He'd hardly spoken to either of his parents since his break-up with Rhea.

Nandini nodded, 'I get it. I wanted to thank you, Saahil.'

'Thank me? For what?' Saahil looked at her quizzically.

He couldn't think of a single thing that she could thank him for. If anything, he'd only been a jerk around her.

'For punching your father,' Nandini said simply. 'A friend of mine witnessed the scene at Four Seasons. She didn't tell me about it for the longest time, of course. All my friends wanted to protect me from the truth about your father. But, when I mentioned my doubts about him being unfaithful to me, she blurted everything out. And it turns out that your father had multiple affairs on the side when we were together. That girl you saw at the hotel wasn't the only one.'

Nandini continued, 'God, I felt so stupid. I get this weird sense of satisfaction from the fact that you punched him.'

Saahil sighed, 'I'm sorry, Nandini. That you had to go through all that.'

She exhaled a deep breath and said, 'Yeah, I'm sorry too. I'm sorry about the fact that I trusted him completely. Anyway, I'm doing much better now. I have a much better perspective on things and moving forward. Things will be good.'

Saahil smiled, 'Good for you.'

Nandini cleared her throat and said, 'Anyway. Enough about my depressing love life. How's your girlfriend? All good?'

Saahil felt his heart sink. 'We broke up a while back. It didn't work out.'

He looked down at the tissue paper on the table and started fiddling with it.

'If you don't mind me asking...what happened? I remember your father mentioning that you were pretty serious about this girl,' Nandini stated.

'My parents happened. I messed up,' Saahil said bluntly.

He didn't know what it was about Nandini, but he wanted to be completely forthcoming with her. He finally wanted to share what had happened with Rhea.

'She wanted me to commit to her...long term. And I couldn't give her that,' Saahil said with no emotion. 'How could I? I am my father's son, after all. I didn't want to spoil her life.'

'Saahil, I hope you don't think this is out of line. But, can

I please say something?' Nandini asked suddenly.

'Sure. Go ahead,' Saahil said.

Their waiter arrived with the cappuccinos and placed it on the table.

'What makes you think that you're going to be the same as your father?' she asked.

It was the same question that Rhea had asked.

'Because that's all I've ever seen, Nandini. I'm scared that my parents have drilled their qualities in me. I've never been a commitment sort of guy. Not till I'd met Rhea, anyway. But marriage...I've seen too much. I've seen and felt too much negativity attached to it,' Saahil explained.

'Okay. I get what you're saying about marriage. Your image has been tarnished. But, Saahil, you need to stop thinking that you're anything like your father. Or even your mother, in fact. I hardly know you, right? And even I can guarantee you that you are nothing like them. You stand up for what's right. You wouldn't have left that night from the restaurant when we were out for dinner, or punched your father, if you were anything like him. You wouldn't have cared! So what if he was with another woman? Big deal. That's his attitude. Not yours. You cared enough to show him what you felt was right or wrong,' Nandini said quietly.

Saahil stared at her and didn't say anything.

Nandini sighed, 'It saddens me to think the impression parents leave on their kids. You're not to blame, Saahil. Anyone in your situation would be the same. But...I'd like to offer you a piece of advice. Get out of this funk.'

Saahil opened his mouth to speak, but she cut him off. 'Your parents are never going to change, right? But, *you* can. As far as I can tell, you want to change. From whatever I know about your family life, you guys have always run away from situations. Don't do that, Saahil. Stop blaming your parents.'

Saahil looked at her in surprise.

'I'm right, aren't I? For whatever has been wrong in your life, you've blamed your parents for it,' Nandini said with a knowing look in her eyes.

Saahil felt like someone had slapped him with a reality check. He'd never even acknowledged this fact about himself and now that someone had said it out loud, it couldn't be more accurate.

'Stop blaming your parents,' Nandini repeated. 'Saahil, it's human nature to blame others for our mistakes. And the blame game works especially in the relationship of a child with their parents. It's the easiest to blame parents for everything. Don't do that. It's your life. You have to make your life decisions yourself. Ultimately, no one else has the right to do that. You're a smart kid, Saahil. Don't let others' actions mark out your future. If your parents are selfish and immature, let them be that. Don't think that you're the same. Because you're not the same. I hardly know you, but that much I have no doubts about.'

Saahil let out a deep breath, 'I don't know what to say.'

'You don't have to say anything. Just think about what I have said. If you think I made any sense…well, you know what to do. You must think that I'm a mad woman who just sat down and started spewing out gyaan. But, I have done a lot of soul searching over the past few months, Saahil, and I've come to realize a few things that I always overlooked earlier. I hope you can find your own happiness, too,' Nandini smiled.

'Thank you, Nandini,' Saahil said with a small smile. 'I wish…someone had told me all this sooner. It's strange, you know? You need someone else to tell you the biggest truth of your life, even though deep down you know it yourself. I've been such a coward. And the messed-up part is that I know I've run away from facing my own problems for as long as I can remember. I've always taken the easy way out. I guess I've needed the affirmation that I'm different from them.'

Nandini nodded.

Saahil gave a harsh laugh, 'Rhea tried to tell me the same thing. But, I was so worked up that night that I couldn't even hear what she was saying. I could have handled things so much differently.'

'You still can, Saahil. It's never too late,' Nandini smiled. 'It sounds like you still really love her.'

Saahil nodded. That was a no-brainer.

Nandini noticed someone waving at her from the other table and got up. 'I wish you all the best, Saahil. I hope things work out,' she said with a final smile and left.

Saahil watched Nandini leave and felt something lifting from his chest.

He felt lighter than he had in years.

He knew exactly what he needed to do.

twenty-eight

Saahil stared at his parents sitting across from him.

They were both stony-faced and looking anywhere but at each other.

Saahil shook his head in amusement.

The moment of epiphany he'd experienced a week ago had changed his entire disposition in life. He couldn't believe that he'd been living under such a façade all these years.

Over the past couple of days, Saahil had caught himself reliving several memories from his childhood and adult life that had made him cringe over the type of person he'd been. Saahil had felt disgusted with himself when he'd remembered a particular incident two–three years after his parents' separation. He'd emotionally manipulated his class teacher into making him pass some of his exams in school because he'd made her believe that he'd been upset about his parents. In reality, Saahil hadn't cared about his exam and had just spent his nights and days partying with his friends, which is why there had been no time to study.

Blaming his parents and their break-up had been the easiest route out of all the sticky situations in his life till now—but not anymore.

Rhea had been right all along.

Saahil let out a small smile at the thought of her.

'What's so funny, Saahil? I don't see any reason for you to smile at this moment,' Manan said coldly. 'Why the hell did you bring us all to Alibaug?'

'Oh, do you need to visit a girlfriend, Manan? We're disturbing your schedule, aren't we?' Payal asked sarcastically.

'Shut up, Payal. You're crazy,' Manan said, still looking straight ahead.

'Suresh! *Ek glass aur Thums Up lao* (Bring me another glass of Thums Up)!' Payal shouted.

There was a flurry of activity from the kitchen, and Saahil saw his mother remove a flask from her purse.

They were at his father's Alibaug house.

Saahil had decided that this was the perfect location to talk to his parents together. There was no way they would ever enter each other's residences, so the Alibaug house had been an apt choice.

Saahil had told them had he wanted to talk to them about something serious, which is why neither of them had put up much of a fight.

They probably thought that he needed to go to rehab for drug addiction and needed their help.

There had been a moment of doubt in Saahil's mind when he'd called his parents to come to Alibaug. He had no idea the way they would react to whatever he had to say.

But that moment of doubt had turned to anger pretty quickly when he'd remembered the past couple of months of his life—he'd been putting off this conversation long enough.

The staff member hurried into the living room with three empty glasses and the soft drink. He set it on the table before hurrying back.

Payal opened her flask and poured vodka into the glass. She mixed it with Thums Up and took a small sip.

'Jesus, Payal. It's 11.00 a.m.,' Manan said in shock.

'It's nice to see how the tables have turned. I would have never imagined you saying this ten years back, Manan,' Payal replied.

She had a smile on her face. She was obviously enjoying provoking her ex-husband and getting a reaction out of him.

'Saahil! Why the hell are we here? I have a very important meeting to get to. And for God's sake, remove those damn sunglasses!' Manan shouted.

'Say it nicely,' Saahil said quietly.

'What?' Manan said.

He seemed confused at Saahil's response.

'Say. It. Nicely,' Saahil repeated slowly. 'That's the only way you'll find out why we're here.'

Manan took a deep breath and exhaled it slowly. 'Saahil… please tell us why we're here,' he said in a much calmer and sugar-coated tone.

Saahil finally removed the black glasses he'd worn since the jetty ride from Mumbai and set them aside. In all honestly, he'd forgotten that he was still wearing them.

'Why are you both so selfish?' Saahil asked quietly.

His parents looked bewildered by his question, as if they had no idea what the word 'selfish' meant. His question had caught them by surprise.

'What do you mean by that, Saahil?' Payal asked.

'You heard me. Why are you both so selfish? I asked you both to come here because I wanted to talk about something important to me, and you guys don't seem to consider it a priority in your life at all,' Saahil said with no expression. 'Dad can't wait to get back to office, and Mom, let's be honest—the only reason you agreed to come is because you would get a chance to provoke Dad and make him angry.'

His parents were staring at him with their mouths hanging open.

'Okay, forget that for a minute. How long has it been since you got divorced?' Saahil asked.

'Eleven years,' Manan said quietly.

'That's right. Eleven years since your divorce and almost thirteen years since you separated. That's a long time, isn't it?' Saahil asked.

Payal's hands were trembling upon hearing Saahil's words. She took a huge sip of her drink.

'What's your point, Saahil?' Manan asked with anger in his eyes.

'My point is…that if it's been so long…why the hell don't you two move on with your respective lives?' Saahil asked.

'Saahil, watch what you're saying!' Manan shouted.

Payal gulped her drink down in a single sip.

'Why? I haven't said anything wrong, have I? Someone needs to tell you guys this or you're going to be stuck in limbo all your lives,' Saahil said, still with no expression.

He was so straight-faced that he felt like he was in a board meeting and droning on and on about boring stuff related to business.

'Dad, I heard Nandini broke up with you,' Saahil stated.

'Um…yes. What does that have to do with all this?' Manan snapped.

'It has everything to do with all this. Why is it that you sabotage all your relationships? You cheated on Nandini several times—even when you proclaimed that you're serious about her,' Saahil said. 'Dad, the reason that you told me for all your affairs and why you do what you do, is absolute bullshit. Mom having an affair all those years ago is not an excuse for you to do this.'

Payal sputtered, 'Wh-How do you...'

Saahil held up a hand. 'Save it, Mom. There's no need for any explanation. I'm not interested.'

He continued, 'So, Mom had an affair. Fine. But then so did you, didn't you? Why are you holding on to it, Dad?' Finally, Saahil felt his voice breaking. He tried to control his emotions and said, 'Nandini was such an amazing person. As much as I hated you being with someone else, you couldn't have found someone better, Dad. You need to open your eyes and your heart. Stop holding on to all that nonsense. You had a real shot at happiness and you blew it.'

Manan was staring at the wall with a mix of emotions on his face. Saahil wasn't sure but he could swear that he saw tears shining in his father's eyes.

'Saahil! How dare you say that in front of me!' Payal screamed. Tears were rolling down her face.

'So what, Mom? So what if I said that? Why don't you two understand that you've been divorced for so long and need to move on in life? Both of you only do stuff to make each angry and hurt. Why? What's the point?' Saahil shouted, his restraint breaking. 'It's clear that you can never be happy together. Why don't you try to be happy without each other, then?'

Payal was sobbing openly now. She opened her flask and took a sip directly from it.

Saahil sighed and wiped a tear from the corner of his eye. He walked over to his mother and took her hands in his. 'Mom. Why do you drink so much? Drinking isn't helping matters, is it? Rather than making yourself stronger, you're making yourself weaker. You should do things that empower you, Mom. Not things that make you lose yourself as a person. You were such a strong person. Go back to that. I get that you're lonely—I totally understand that. Find stuff that keeps you busy, Mom. Go back to the fashion world! Open a boutique again! There's so much you can do!'

His mother looked at him in surprise through her tears.

'Hell, why are you sitting at home all alone? You're a young and beautiful woman. Go out there and date! What's stopping you?' Saahil exclaimed.

Payal shook her head, 'It's not so easy, Saahil.'

Saahil got up from next to his mother and looked at her with a hard expression, 'Yeah, well, toughen up. If you can't do it for yourself, do it for *me*.'

His parents looked at him in shock.

'Have you both ever stopped and considered what your relationship has done to me? Done to your only child? Do you have any idea how messed-up and cynical it has made me? I never got into a serious relationship earlier because I had so many trust issues. I *still* have so many trust issues. I always expect the worst out of people. Dad, instead of telling me that commitment is a wonderful thing, you advised me to never commit to anyone. Well, thanks, Dad. I sabotaged my relationship with Rhea partly because of your advice,' Saahil said harshly.

He wiped another tear from his eye.

He took a deep breath and continued, 'Why is it that it's always me who has to deal with your bullshit? When have either of you sacrificed your life for me? Can you think of a time when I came to you for help and you helped me out? No. You were so involved in your tumultuous relationship when I was a kid that you forgot that I even existed. Can you even begin to imagine what that did to me? I spent years thinking my parents don't give a shit about me. I still think that. I've developed such a defence mechanism now, that these things don't bother me a lot anymore. However, when Rhea broke up with me…it broke me as a person. And neither of you were there for me, even then. When am I going to be a priority in your life? It's my time now! I messed up the only important thing in my life because I always thought I'm like the both of you—that I would screw up as well. You set such an amazing example, guys. You both need to move on from your baggage and let me move on as well!'

Payal was sobbing uncontrollably while Manan was still staring at the wall.

Saahil let out a breath and said, 'While I realized that I shouldn't blame my parents for my misgivings, there was still a nagging thought in the back of my head. It said that my parents need to move on as well in order for me to completely let go of my demons. That's why I called you here today.'

Saahil felt unbelievably exhausted and sat down on the sofa.

With her hands trembling, Payal picked up her flask and went into the kitchen.

Saahil could hear her pouring something into the sink.

'Saahil…I know it doesn't count for anything, but I just emptied the flask into the sink. I'm going to be better, son. I'm so sorry,' Payal said as she re-entered the room. She bent at the knees and sat on the floor, with her face in her hands.

Saahil walked over to her and pulled her up. 'That's all I'm asking, Mom. I'm asking you to try and not give up. Just… let go, Mom. I promise to be there to catch you if you fall.'

His mother looked up and stared at him with a wondrous expression on her face. It was as if she was seeing him for the first time in a very long time.

Manan finally cleared his throat and got up as well.

Saahil saw him open his mouth to speak, but Manan didn't say anything.

They stared at each other for a couple of seconds, before Manan lowered his gaze.

But it wasn't before Saahil glimpsed shining tears in his eyes.

Saahil gave his parents a small smile.

It was the first time, in a very long time that they'd spoken openly to each other as a family.

'Saahil!' Payal cried out in anguish. 'You must make things right with Rhea, beta. She's a wonderful girl. *We'll* make things right.'

Saahil felt his throat close up. 'I'm afraid it's too late for that, Mom. A friend of mine told me that she's started dating someone else. I'm scared…I'm scared that I've lost the love of my life, Mom.'

twenty-nine

'Thanks for tonight. I'll call you…' Rhea said.

'Yeah, sounds great,' Punit smiled at her as they sat in his car below Rhea's building. 'I had a really good time.'

'Likewise. Goodnight,' Rhea said quickly and stepped out of the car.

She waited till he drove off and then let out a sigh of relief.

That had been the most boring three hours of her life.

A colleague that had started working for Rhea's brand had set her up on a date with Punit. While he seemed like a nice guy, he was also so boring that Rhea had felt like shooting herself by the end of their date.

She sighed and walked toward the elevator.

Punit had gone on and on about his job at an accounting firm. Rhea had tried to seem interested in what he was saying, but could barely keep her eyes open.

Rhea's phone pinged. She saw that it was a text message from Punit:

```
Good night! Please let's do this again soon!
```

Rhea groaned.

There was no way in hell that she was going out with him ever again.

She ignored the message and pressed the button to her floor when the elevator doors opened.

The worst part of the night had been when Punit had eyed her non-vegetarian food with judgement. Since he'd stuck with vegetarian options, Rhea had figured that Punit was a pure shakahari.

Not that there was anything wrong with that.

He just didn't have to judge her dietary choices.

Rhea opened the door to her apartment and walked in. 'Mom, I'm home!'

Simran rushed to the entrance of the apartment. 'Hi, beta! How was the date?'

Rhea snorted, 'Don't even ask. It was so bad that I don't have the energy to describe it.'

Simran crossed her arms over her chest and leaned against the wall. 'What was wrong with him?'

'He was just…really boring,' Rhea said.

She walked into the living room and sat down on the couch. 'What movie did you watch tonight, Mom?'

'That's it? He was boring?' Simran asked, ignoring her question.

Rhea looked at her mother weirdly. 'Yes, Mom. That's it.'

'That's not enough of a reason to not date him. You'll grow to like him,' Simran said as she joined Rhea on the couch.

'Well…there was just no connection there. You know what I mean? I could barely stay awake throughout dinner. I was that bored. Besides, he was eyeing my food all weirdly. He had an aversion to me eating non-vegetarian food, I think,' Rhea explained.

Simran just stared at Rhea, not saying anything.

'What? What's wrong? Do I have something on my face?' Rhea asked.

'Nope. Just wondering if I should have *the talk* with you

right now or later,' Simran said quietly.

'Talk? What talk? And right now, Mom. Please don't keep me in suspense,' Rhea exclaimed.

'Fine,' Simran said. 'I guess now's as good a time as any. How many guys have you been on dates with over the past couple of months?'

'Um…Let me think,' Rhea scrunched up her face. 'Five, I think.'

'And you found something wrong with each and every one of them. Fine, this guy sounds crazy if he found something wrong with you for eating non-vegetarian food, but what about the others? You didn't feel the "connection" with any of them either,' Simran commented.

'Well, yes. There was just no spark, Mom,' Rhea said.

She really didn't understand why her mother was going down this path.

'Rhea,' Simran sighed. 'You know the real reason why you haven't felt a spark with any of them? It's because of Saahil. You're still hung up on him.'

'Mom!' Rhea shouted as she sprang up from the couch. 'I'm not hung up on him. Sure, I miss him at times, but that's about it! I'm trying to move on!'

'Yes, beta, I know you're trying to move on. But, deep down, you still love him, which is why you can't seem to open your mind or your heart to someone else!' Simran said.

'Mom,' Rhea said quietly. 'It takes time to move on. Even if what you are saying is true, what's even the point? Saahil and I wanted different things. I *still* want a commitment from him—something that he won't be able to give. So, there's no point to this conversation. That chapter of my life is over.'

'Rhea, come sit down,' Simran patted the seat next to her.

'I want to tell you something.'

Rhea sighed dejectedly and sat down next to her mother. Her spirits were falling and she felt a wave of sadness wash over her.

'Your father and I met in college, and it was love at first sight,' Simran said fondly. 'We were so in love and so happy. Our lives were planned together, and we were over the moon with joy. When you came into this world—we knew that our lives were complete. We didn't need anything else.'

Rhea felt tears pricking her eyes 'I miss him, Mom.'

'I miss him too. When your father passed away…I didn't know what to do, Rhea. I felt so helpless and lonely. My soulmate had left me,' Simran explained. Her voice was heavy with grief now. 'Our life plan had been altered. What I'm trying to tell you, beta, is that life is unexpected. Nothing is set in stone. We may think that we have life figured out, but that's not true.'

Rhea didn't say anything. She missed her father so much.

'Rhea, I know you love Saahil. A lot. And I don't blame you—he's a wonderful boy. But, he's been through his own hell. He may have seen and heard stuff that actually scarred him for life. We can't even begin to imagine the stuff he must have gone through, beta. His take on relationships must be so screwed up, thanks to his parents,' Simran explained.

Rhea nodded, 'I know.'

'Even then, his philosophy in life is so wonderful. He sticks up for what is right and wrong, from whatever you've told me. Some people actually go insane after such a rocky childhood, but he kept his sanity. That's saying something, beta. Sure, we went through our own hell when we lost your father, but that doesn't mean we can discount Saahil's grief. To live everyday knowing that your parents can't stand the sight of each other and don't give a damn about their child is hell in itself, Rhea,' Simran stated.

Rhea felt a drop of tear hit her cheek.

Simran took a deep breath and said, 'I know you wanted the ultimate commitment from him. At the end of the day, everyone wants that. Especially women. We've been brought up in such a way that marriage is the final destination of a relationship. It's just how things are done. But, Rhea…why do you have to follow something just because it's what everyone else does?'

Rhea looked up at her mother with a confused expression. 'Mom, what do you mean? Everyone gets married!'

'That's exactly my point! Everyone does get married—but it doesn't mean that you need to get married as well. Your happiness lies in being with Saahil, not by some ritual that says that you're married forever. As I said earlier, Rhea, nothing is set in stone. Even if you're married, it doesn't guarantee that you'll be happy forever, right? Life is all about taking chances. Why do you need a piece of paper saying you're husband and wife to be happy?' Simran asked.

Rhea shook her head. 'Hold on, Mom. I can't think straight. All my friends are slowly getting hitched. I mean, I always thought that I'd be in the same boat, you know? You're right, I do love Saahil and I've been trying to forget him, but it's not been successful. However, I don't know how to completely forego the idea of marriage!'

'Rhea,' Simran said quietly. 'I never thought that your father will pass away and I'll be left all alone. But, it did happen. That's what life is. It tests you and your strength. I was so angry at life. It had taken away my happiness. I always thought that my happiness lies only with your father. But, Rhea, it took me time to understand that I still have so much to be grateful and happy for. I have you with me. I'm healthy. There are so many people out there who aren't healthy and are suffering. At least I don't have to go through all of that. I had to find my own happiness again, Rhea.'

'Mom...' Rhea began.

'Rhea, just hear me out,' Simran interrupted. 'I'll give you two options right now, and you'll have to choose between the two. You won't have time to think. Is that okay?'

Rhea nodded yes.

'Rhea, what do you choose between Saahil and marriage?' Simran asked.

Rhea felt her heart stop.

It was the moment of truth.

She heard herself say, 'Saahil.'

Simran smiled, 'Finally, you're being honest with yourself. Beta, if you love him so much, don't hold back on something that makes you so happy. I've seen you over the past couple of months, Rhea. You're miserable. I thought that with time, it'll be better, but I haven't seen you come out of this. Sure, you've been trying, but you've always just tried to find *him* in someone else. That is simply not possible, Rhea. There's only one Saahil, isn't there? So what if you don't end up getting married? Saahil is the one who will complete your life—if he won't be in your life, what's even the point of anything? *He* is your happiness, Rhea. Nothing else.'

Rhea let out the breath that she'd been holding in. 'I don't even know where things stand between us anymore, Mom. He's tried to contact me several times, but I've never responded. How can I just waltz back into his life?'

'You'll figure it out,' Simran said.

'What if he can't give me any sort of commitment, Mom? He used to have so many girlfriends before he met me. I don't know how...' Rhea left the statement hanging in the air.

'He was an amazing boyfriend to you, wasn't he?' Simran asked smilingly.

Rhea felt a tug on her heart. 'Yes. Yes, he was.'

'You didn't expect him to be one, but he surprised you. So don't be sure to pass judgement on him, Rhea. He might just be completely different. You have to take a risk at some point. If he's worth it, what's wrong in a bit of a gamble? There are no guarantees about anything, beta. You have to go all in or nothing,' Simran explained.

Rhea looked at her mother with a hopeful expression, 'I don't know, Mom. Are you sure?'

'I'm positive, Rhea. I know you. You won't be happy otherwise. Your happiness is with Saahil, and it's time you stop running away from it!' Simran exclaimed.

Rhea let out a huge breath. 'Thanks, Mom. I don't know what I would do without you.'

Simran laughed as well. 'Oh, please. You've known everything that I've just told you. You just needed someone to say it to you. And I'll always be there for that, Rhea.'

Rhea plopped back on the couch.

She felt a surge of hope within her...a feeling of being revived all over again.

It felt like months had passed without her feeling any sort of happiness.

Her mother was right. She'd been trying to deny her feelings for Saahil, but it was time she stopped running away from it.

She picked up her phone and stared at it.

She almost dialled Saahil's number, but there was so much that needed to be said that a mere phone call just wouldn't suffice in this situation.

It felt impersonal.

This had to be done the right way.

thirty

'Sagar, I don't care,' Saahil frowned at his assistant. 'I need this document to clear immediately.'

'Sir, it's just taking a bit longer than expected—'

'That's not my concern,' Saahil retorted. 'Make it happen.'

His conversation was interrupted by the sound of his phone ringing. Saahil saw that it was Abhishek calling.

Saahil ignored the call and looked back at Sagar. His assistant looked extremely apprehensive.

Perhaps because he knew Saahil had been in a foul mood all day.

There was no particular reason for this mood—Saahil had just woken up feeling angry at the world.

'Sir, I'll get right on it. I'm sorry for the delay,' Sagar said quickly.

Saahil nodded and looked back at his computer screen. This was the cue for Sagar to leave and he left from his boss' cabin in a hurry.

Saahil sighed. He felt like a jerk at work sometimes. It really wasn't like him to be so stern around people.

His phone rang again.

'Hey. What's up?' Saahil said to Abhishek as he picked up.

'Saahil. Sorry if I'm disturbing you, bro. But, there's something that needs your attention,' Abhishek replied urgently.

'What's wrong?' Saahil asked, confused.

'You need to go by your old house. I saw several lights on in there on my way home. Not kidding. Since it's on my way back home from work, I always see it embedded in darkness. However, that wasn't the case today. Someone needs to go check it out!' Abhishek exclaimed.

Saahil sighed, 'Abhishek, that's not possible. No one stays there except a caretaker. And I'm pretty sure he would know whether there are uninvited guests there.'

Feeling extremely exhausted, Saahil got up from his seat and stretched. He checked his watch and saw that it was after 8.00 p.m. He was looking forward to going home and sleeping.

This day needed to end.

Now, if only Abhishek would let go of this notion that someone was taking advantage of his empty residence, all would be well.

'Saahil, man. Just go check it out. What's the harm in that? You'll be grateful that I let you know of a potential burglary beforehand!' Abhishek said.

He did have a point.

As much as he was looking forward to crashing on his bed, Saahil would always hold himself responsible if someone had broken into his childhood home, and he hadn't done anything about it.

'Fine,' Saahil said into the phone. 'I'll go by and check if everything is fine. You happy?'

'Ecstatic, bro. I'm ecstatic,' Abhishek said happily and hung up.

Saahil called for his bag to be put into his car, and turned on some music as soon as he got into his Range Rover. Coldplay soared through the car, and he was soon on his way to Pedder Road.

After fifteen minutes of swerving through traffic, he finally reached his old driveway.

What the fuck?

Abhishek had been right.

He could see several lights from within the house.

Saahil quickly got out of his car and shouted, 'Watchman!'

There was no answer.

Saahil looked around him but couldn't see anything out of the ordinary.

Maybe the housekeeper who came to clean the house every week had left the lights on by mistake.

Saahil inched closer to the front gate and turned the knob.

He was greeted by darkness.

However, once he ran his eyes over the dark hallway, Saahil saw a dim light coming from over the staircase.

With his heart beating thousand miles a minute, Saahil climbed the staircase.

A confused expression came over his face as he reached the top stair.

There were candles lit in the hallway leading to his old bedroom.

What in the world is going on?

He followed the candles and they stopped right in front of his room. Saahil opened the door and his heart skipped several beats.

Rhea was standing in the middle of his room, with a shy smile on her face.

She was the most beautiful thing he'd ever seen.

'Rhea? What...I don't understand...' Saahil started.

All he wanted to do was take her in his arms, but he controlled himself.

'Hi,' Rhea said quietly.

Saahil looked around the room and noticed that his bedroom was still exactly the same as he'd left it since his last visit. The only difference was Rhea.

His room had never looked better.

Saahil took a step toward her and said, 'How are you?'

'Good,' Rhea said while fidgeting with her hands. 'How are you?'

'Good as well,' Saahil replied.

He hated the fact that they were being so formal around each other. It was funny how things changed.

Rhea said quickly, 'I made Abhishek call you to make sure you came here. Since he was the only one I'd properly met when…we…were together…I called him.'

Saahil took a step toward her. He had so much to say to her.

'That's okay. I spoke to my parents, Rhea,' he said quickly. 'I'm sorry that I'm interrupting you, but I need to get it off my chest. I'm sorry, Rhea. I've been such an idiot. You were right to break-up with me. I didn't deserve you. You're such an amazing person…and I'm nowhere close to that.'

Rhea started to close the distance between them, but Saahil held up a hand. 'Please. Let me finish.'

Rhea stopped in her tracks and nodded.

'After you broke up with me, I was miserable. I still *am* miserable. However, it took me a while to understand that you were right all along. I was wrong to compare myself to my parents, Rhea. I'm not like them, and it was stupid of me to think that I would turn out to be like them. I've been blaming them for all my misgivings over the years, when the truth is that I've been shying away from my own responsibilities,' Saahil said.

He could see tears shining in Rhea's eyes.

'My app idea is in the process of being taken over by a Bangalore company,' Saahil said conversationally. 'They loved the idea. Do you know what I wanted to do when I found out?'

Rhea shook her head.

Her hair fell over her eye, and Saahil's fingers itched to touch them.

'I wanted to call you and tell you the news. You were the only person I wanted to call, Rhea. It made me realize that I was so dumb to let you go away,' Saahil said simply.

'Saahil…' Rhea said.

'Hold on. I'm not done yet,' Saahil shook his head. 'Back to my original statement. I spoke to my parents. I spoke to them more openly that I've ever spoken to them. I opened my heart to them, Rhea. It made me feel lighter than I've ever felt. I told my father to grow the hell up and not be such an asshole anymore. And my mother…I told her that she should quit drinking and do something that makes her stronger, not weaker. Rhea, for the first time ever, they *heard* me. I don't know if they'll ever follow through, but at least I did my part. I told them what I feel. The rest is up to them.'

'I'm so proud of you, Saahil,' Rhea whispered.

Tears were rolling down her cheeks.

Saahil couldn't control himself any longer. He went up to her and wiped her cheek with the back of his hand.

'Shit,' he said, taking his hand away. 'I'm sorry. I know you're dating someone else. I shouldn't have done that.'

A strange expression came over Rhea's face. 'What are you talking about?'

'You have a new boyfriend,' Saahil said simply.

Rhea shook her head. 'Saahil, I'm not dating anyone.'

A spark of hope lit in Saahil's heart. 'You're not?'

Rhea gave a short laugh, 'No, I'm not. Not that I didn't try. I tried very hard to move on, Saahil. But you're like a parasite that's stuck inside my heart. As much as I tried to get rid of you, I just couldn't do it!'

Saahil gave a small smile, 'Really?'

'Yes, really,' Rhea said. 'I went on several dates over the past few months, but they all went horribly. They were all really nice guys as well.'

Saahil's smile faltered a bit.

'But, I was just trying to find Saahil Kapoor in each and every one of them. That's just not possible, is it?' Rhea asked.

Saahil slowly shook his head. He still didn't know whether to be happy with her proclamation or not.

'I'm the one who is dumb, Saahil. I didn't understand where you were coming from. I know you went through hell your entire childhood. Anyone in your situation would act like you did. Even though you saw and heard so much crap, you still turned out to be a wonderful human being. That's what is important! The fact that you went and confronted your parents makes you such a strong person, Saahil. I can't even begin to tell you how proud I am,' Rhea said tenderly.

She took a step toward him and stroked his cheek.

'I don't need marriage, Saahil. I don't need it at all. I just need you in my life,' Rhea whispered.

Saahil shook his head, 'Rhea... Why should you compromise on what is so important to you? I've felt like killing myself over the past few months that I can't give you what you want. I wish I could get married. But...I've just begun the road to recovery. It's going to be a long and rocky process.'

Saahil cleared his throat. He could feel his emotions getting the better of him. He couldn't believe that he was pushing Rhea away again.

'Saahil,' Rhea said firmly. 'Listen to me. I do not want to get married. I did want to, but not anymore. I can say it over a thousand times if that's what it will take for you to believe me. All I need is you in my life. That's what matters. If I have you by my side, what else do I need? Marriage is all about being with each other in times of happiness and sadness. If I don't have you at all...how the hell am I going to be happy? *You* are my happiness, Saahil Kapoor.'

Saahil whispered, 'Are you sure?'

Rhea smiled, 'Yes.'

Saahil heard himself rush through his words. 'I'll never leave you, Rhea. I promise. I've missed you so much...I just can't believe...I wasn't sure...'

'Ssshh,' Rhea held a finger to Saahil's lips. 'I love you.'

Saahil's face broke out in a relieved smile. 'I love you too. I've been going crazy waiting for you to say that, Rhea.'

Saahil reached out to pull her toward him, but Rhea stepped out of his way.

'There's just one thing left to do,' she said.

An unsure expression came over her face, and Saahil could feel a million thoughts going through her mind.

He'd come to know what her expressions meant over the years.

'Rhea? What's wrong?' Saahil asked in a panicked voice.

'Saahil, I wanted to do this in your old bedroom, since I know how much sentimental value you attach to it,' Rhea said with a small smile. 'This is where it all began for you, and it's time you attach a happy memory to this place. At least, I hope it will be a happy memory.'

Saahil didn't say anything. He didn't know where she was going with this.

Suddenly, Rhea bent down on one knee.

She took a box out of her jeans pocket and opened it.

Inside was a metal key.

Saahil looked at her in surprise.

'Saahil Kapoor,' Rhea said, looking up at him. 'Will you move in with me?'

Saahil's face broke out into a huge smile—a smile that soon turned into the most genuine laugh that he'd had in a while.

He pulled Rhea to her feet.

Just before his lips met hers, Saahil whispered, 'Yes.'

Epilogue

Six Months Later

'Simran ji, I can't even begin to describe what a terror Saahil was as a kid!' Payal exclaimed.

'Really?' Simran asked, a surprised expression on her face. 'I can't imagine Saahil being a terror! He's such a gentleman!'

'Oh, trust me. He was an absolute badmaash,' Manan stated.

'Guys,' Saahil interjected. 'Please stop. There's no need to hash up such embarrassing details of my childhood!'

'No, wait! I definitely need to know these stories!' Rhea said laughingly.

They were all seated in Rhea and Saahil's apartment on Nepean Sea Road.

The last six months had gone by in a blur.

The apartment that Rhea had found for them to live in was a delight—it was cozy and just spacious enough for two people.

Rhea had finally reached the point of satisfaction with the way the apartment was set up, and they had decided to call their respective parents for dinner for the very first time.

'Rhea,' Saahil sighed. 'Don't encourage them.'

'Oh, please,' Payal huffed. 'As if we need any encouragement to talk about your childhood, beta.'

Saahil noticed that his mother's wine glass was untouched. He hid his smile from the crowd.

'So, Saahil and a couple of his classmates used to go to this Math teacher's apartment for private tuitions after school. Rhea, Saahil was a terrible student, let me just say that. All his school teachers were fed up with him. Anyway, this tuition teacher wasn't very strict, and these boys definitely took advantage of that. Once, the Math teacher fell really sick, and he had all these homoeopathy tiny bottles in his apartment. The boys obviously found out that he wasn't feeling very well. During one of the study sessions, their teacher told them that he was stepping out of the apartment for a few minutes and the boys should continue with their work. Saahil, obviously, took this as the perfect indication to misbehave. He convinced all his friends to empty the teacher's homoeopathy bottles and to pee in them!' Payal described animatedly.

'What!' Rhea exclaimed. 'Yuck! That's sick, Saahil.'

Simran looked at Saahil in horror and then burst out laughing.

Saahil tried to control his grin, but gave up in the end. 'I'd totally forgotten about that, Mom. Man, I got such a beating from that teacher that day.'

'You deserved it, Saahil! Didn't he get into trouble with a lot of his other teachers as well, Payal?' Manan asked his ex-wife.

'Yes. Yes, he did. Do you remember how he convinced his Science tuition teacher to forget about studying and play table tennis with him instead?' Payal said with a laugh.

Manan laughed as well. 'Yes, you're right. I had to fire that guy.'

Saahil looked at his parents with the secret smile again.

Their hostility toward each other seemed to be at the bare

minimum. He wasn't sure, but they actually seemed to be getting along.

'Okay, hold on. I'll be right back. I need to bring out the appetizers,' Rhea said as she got up.

'I'll come help you,' Saahil said quickly.

He followed Rhea into their tiny kitchen and grabbed her by the waist. 'Do you regret moving in with such a delinquent, Ms Singh?'

Rhea laughed as she placed her hands on his chest. 'Not at all. I love hearing about your childhood. You know that. As disgusting as some of the stories might be.'

Saahil smiled, 'Stuff seems to be going well outside, right? They all seem to be getting along—including my parents.'

Rhea kissed Saahil's cheek tenderly. 'Yes. I'm happy to see that you're happy.'

'I don't want to jinx it...but I'm really happy, Rhea,' Saahil whispered. 'Thank you. For...taking this chance with me.'

'I love you, Saahil. Thank *you* for giving me the best six months of my life,' Rhea smiled. 'Now, go back outside. I'll be there soon.'

Saahil walked back to where everyone was seated, and saw that it was Simran's turn to narrate one of Rhea's stories.

'Rhea was such a difficult child,' Simran put her hands on her forehead. 'Remember when Benetton was such a craze at one time? Well, I decided to shop for Rhea from Benetton, when she was five–six years old, I think. Rhea loved those T-shirts so much, that she only wore them for over a month. She didn't let anyone wash them! In fact, it wasn't that she just wore one T-shirt continuously—she wore two t-shirts at once. One on top of the other. I finally had to throw away those two t-shirts secretly so that she would let go of them.'

Saahil hooted with laughter as Rhea came back to the room with a tray in her hands.

'Mom! You can't tell them these things!' Rhea said with a horrified expression.

Saahil took the tray from her hands and set it on the table as everyone burst out laughing.

He looked sideways at Rhea as she sat down next to him.

He couldn't believe that he'd gotten everything he'd ever wanted.

She'd caught him and did not let go.

Acknowledgements

This book wouldn't have been possible without the guidance of my husband, Raghav. You are the constant pillar of support and love in my life. Thank you for bearing with my oscillating mind.

Thank you to all my friends and family members who have helped me reach this wonderful chapter. I'm extremely grateful to all the people who went through my manuscript and gave me their suggestions.

Thank you to my agent, Suhail Mathur, and the entire team of The Book Bakers for believing in my writing capabilities.

Thank you to Rupa Publications for publishing me.